"You aren't goin

"What makes you say

"The way you look at me. I'm not mad. It just would have been a dream job."

"You're kidding."

"No. I adore kids, especially yours." Sherry ducked her head with a vulnerability that caught Rafe off guard.

One thing he believed—she genuinely liked his niece and nephew.

"I can't afford to pay a lot anyway." What had made him say that?

"I'm aware that nannies don't rank high on the wage scale." She wrapped her arms around her knees, keeping her slender legs angled away from him. "Since you *aren't* my boss, I'm going to offer a suggestion."

"You're handing out parenting advice?"

"In your case, yes."

Dear Reader,

In creating the stories set in Harmony Circle, I undertook the ticklish task of creating a character who seemed unsympathetic in earlier books but now steps forward as a heroine.

Sherry LaSalle is an heiress who unintentionally insulted a great many people, and now has to live among them—without her fortune. She faces her greatest challenge in making peace with neighbor Rafe Montoya, a brooding mechanic who considers her a hopeless snob.

Having clipped coupons and lived on a budget all my life, I had fun imagining my world through the eyes of this once-privileged young woman. She's never shopped in a discount store or kept track of credit-card charges, let alone applied for a job.

But Sherry won me over with her can-do spirit, and she wins over Rafe, as well. I hope you enjoy her story!

Best,

Jacqueline Diamond

Million-Dollar Nanny

JACQUELINE DIAMOND

TORONTO • NEW YORK • LONDON
AMSTERDAM • PARIS • SYDNEY • HAMBURG
STOCKHOLM • ATHENS • TOKYO • MILAN • MADRID
PRAGUE • WARSAW • BUDAPEST • AUCKLAND

Recycling programs
for this product may
not exist in your area.

ISBN-13: 978-0-373-75246-1
ISBN-10: 0-373-75246-6

MILLION-DOLLAR NANNY

This edition published by arrangement with Harlequin Books S.A.

www.eHarlequin.com

Printed in U.S.A.

ABOUT THE AUTHOR

Jacqueline Diamond and her husband have raised two sons in a Southern California community much like Harmony Circle. In between driving car pools and helping her kids prepare for college, she's written eighty novels, ranging from fantasy to mystery and romance. Jackie enjoys gardening, reading and hearing from readers at jdiamondfriends@yahoo.com. You can keep up with her latest news on her Web site, www.jacquelinediamond.com.

Books by Jacqueline Diamond

HARLEQUIN AMERICAN ROMANCE

913—THE IMPROPERLY PREGNANT PRINCESS
962—DIAGNOSIS: EXPECTING BOSS'S BABY
971—PRESCRIPTION: MARRY HER IMMEDIATELY
978—PROGNOSIS: A BABY? MAYBE
1046—THE BABY'S BODYGUARD
1075—THE BABY SCHEME
1094—THE POLICE CHIEF'S LADY*
1101—NINE-MONTH SURPRISE*
1109—A FAMILY AT LAST*
1118—DAD BY DEFAULT*
1130—THE DOCTOR + FOUR*
1149—THE DOCTOR'S LITTLE SECRET
1163—DADDY PROTECTOR
1177—TWIN SURPRISE
1209—THE FAMILY NEXT DOOR†
1223—BABY IN WAITING†

*Downhome Doctors
†Harmony Circle

To my loyal readers, new and old

Chapter One

Pants on backward. Jelly smeared on his nose. And hair sticking up as if… Yep, that had grape jelly on it, too.

"How'd you manage to get a faceful of jam?" Rafe Montoya asked, hauling his four-year-old nephew into the bathroom and hoisting him onto the counter. "I fixed you guys cereal for breakfast."

"I hate that kind of cereal." Juan, a stocky tyke with eyes almost as dark as Rafe's, folded his arms defiantly as his uncle rubbed a washcloth across his scrunched face.

"You asked for that brand." Or had he? Maybe it was his twin sister, Sofia, who adored graham-cracker-flavored cereal, Rafe conceded while he tackled the hair. It was impossible to get clean. Slightly less sticky was the best he could do. "Anyway, it wouldn't kill you to be a good sport."

Juan thudded a sneaker-clad heel against the shelf below him. "Mom used to make us tortillas and jam for breakfast."

"I'm out of tortillas."

Rafe supposed this mess was partly his own fault, for failing to supervise breakfast. He'd been interrupted by a phone call from his chief mechanic, Mario Stenopolous, who'd opened the garage early and called with the good news that parts had finally arrived for Sherry LaSalle's luxury sedan.

Rafe had told him to tackle that job straightaway. The sooner they got his snobby new neighbor off their backs, the better.

What really grated was that he had to do the job for free. That was cheaper than hiring a lawyer to fight *her* lawyer, who insisted the mess was all Rafe's fault.

Two months ago, he'd finished repairing the engine and had handed the keys to Sherry's fiancé, an arrogant jerk named Winston Grooms III, believing the man was collecting it on her behalf. Instead, the man had fled just before an FBI investigation began, abandoning the car—stripped of removable parts—at the Las Vegas airport.

Rafe got stuck restoring it, while Sherry, whose fortune Winston had scammed, now lived across the street from Rafe in a cottage she'd once planned to tear down and replace with an ugly mansion. Oh, to heck with the woman. He had more important matters to think about this morning, like getting his recently adopted niece and nephew ready for day care.

"Unc' Rafe?" Sofia appeared in the bathroom doorway. The kid had a talent for sneaking up on him. "Brush my hair?"

"Didn't I do that already?" He lowered Juan, who bolted for the hallway, narrowly missing his sister.

She shook her head at Rafe. Her dark hair was tangled—and full of graham-cracker crumbs.

Apparently she'd mussed it with her own little hands. The kid craved contact and attention. Reminding himself of how much she'd been through, Rafe retrieved her brush and set to work. Again.

Until the previous summer, he'd survived more than thirty years of living without once untangling a little girl's locks or scrubbing a preschooler's face. Aside from buying gifts for the twins and playing with them during family get-togethers, he'd left them to the doting care of his younger brother, Manuel, and sister-in-law, Cara.

But last summer, a brush fire had swept the estate north of Los Angeles where they'd worked, killing them and the horses they'd been trying to rescue. Fortunately the twins, who had been celebrating their fourth birthday, were spending the night with their grandparents.

Afterward, when ill health sidelined the elder members of the family, Rafe stepped in to claim the orphans. Still, even after the adoption ceremony in April had transformed Rafe into an instant dad, he felt lost at sea. How was he supposed to handle Juan's rebellious streak and Sofia's clinginess? He could only do his clumsy best day by day.

"Okay, guys," Rafe announced. "Grab those backpacks."

Juan grumbled, and Sofia made a valiant attempt to wrap herself around her uncle's leg. Luckily they only had a short walk to the neighbor's home day care center.

Outside, clouds dimmed the Southern California sky. During June, the sun typically didn't break through until afternoon here in Brea, a cozy shopping mecca in inland Orange County.

On the porch, Rafe locked the door before escorting the children down the walk. Hardly a breath of wind stirred the palm trees that fronted his stucco home. A gardening truck rumbled by, the only traffic on this lower curve of Harmony Road.

The U-shaped street, which held slightly fewer than twenty homes, lay at the heart of a 350-unit development called Harmony Circle. Rafe loved his comfortable, friendly neighborhood. He wasn't exactly glad Winston had absconded with Sherry's money, particularly since the thief had ripped off many of her friends, too. But thank goodness Rafe didn't have to worry about her building an oversize monstrosity across the street anymore. Rafe had led the fight to preserve her charming cottage, one of a pair of 1920s bungalows that predated the rest of the development by over half a century.

"Oh, look." Sofia released a fluttery breath. "It's the princess."

She was staring at a petite figure emerging from Sherry's cottage. A frothy pink dress swirled around his new neighbor as her high heels tapped down the steps from her porch. A ray of sunlight pierced the clouds, turning her blond hair—today done up in a twist—to spun gold.

He had to admit the twenty-seven-year-old former prima donna of Orange County society still looked like a million bucks as she marched toward the aging vehicle Rafe had been forced to lend her. Despite her proud posture, he noted a hint of vulnerability in the set of her mouth, and felt a twinge of sympathy. Living among residents she'd offended, and being reduced to pinching pennies must be tough on the young woman.

Then, as she slid behind the wheel, she glanced toward him. Through the glare on the windshield, he saw a sneer distort her pretty face.

"Princess is right," he muttered.

"I thought she was a witch," Juan piped.

Rafe had privately referred to his neighbor that way more than once during the heated battle over the cottage. "Come on, guys. Can't you hear the cars waiting for me at the garage? They're rumbling and smoking and spelling out my name."

"Can she do magic spells?" Juan asked doggedly as they swung left toward the nursery.

"If she could, she'd summon that creep of a fiancé from whatever hole he's hiding in." Rafe had summarized the situation for the children by saying her boyfriend had run off with her money. He wondered if he should have explained more or avoided the topic altogether. It was hard to tell how kids perceived things.

"Does she have a fairy wand?" Sofia asked dreamily.

"Maybe. She's pretty good at making men disappear." Before the debacle with the now-infamous Winston, whose real name was Wally Grinnell, Sherry had landed in the news with her divorce from the wealthy older attorney she'd married when she was nineteen. Not only had she raked in vast alimony, she'd received an already substantial inheritance from her parents.

Published estimates gave her former worth as ten million dollars, all gone thanks to her "fiancé." How ironic that Rafe, a mechanic who'd struggled to afford this house and to buy his own business, now had more money than the woman who used to look down her nose at people like him.

Judging by her expression a moment ago, she still did.

He guided the children across the street and past the second cottage, which belonged to octogenarian Minnie

Ortiz. At the stucco home next door to hers, he heard the happy noise of youngsters at play.

Sofia gripped Rafe's hand. "You'll be fine," he told her as they waited for the owner to answer the bell. "You *like* Mrs. Hughes and her kids."

"I want to go home," Sofia whimpered.

"You will. As soon as I'm done working."

"Our real home."

"We have to make the best of things." How long before the children accepted their loss? Rafe didn't mean to ask too much of them, but just wished there was a way he could put all their painful memories behind them.

Maryam Hughes, an elegant, dark-skinned woman in her early forties, admitted them with a strained smile. As the children ran past, she addressed Rafe. "Could you step inside for a moment? I need to speak with you."

"Sure." Uneasily, he recalled that Juan had had a squabble the other day with Maryam's little boy, Luther. Rafe had hoped the whole thing would blow over.

Maryam got her charges settled in the den. There were six, including her pair and two other girls. Although the room seemed filled with screeching, wiggling bodies, his hostess skillfully sorted the kids and started them on coloring projects.

"Sorry for the delay." She accompanied him to the living room, which was furnished with an eclectic blend of ethnic pieces and antiques. "I'm afraid I have bad news."

"Is your husband all right?" J. J. Hughes, a college history professor, had seemed fine when he'd played softball with Rafe on Saturday.

"Yes, but my mother isn't." Tension marked her usually composed face. "She suffered a stroke last weekend. It's mild as these things go, but she'll require a lot of care over the next few months. After the hospital releases her on Friday, she'll be moving in with us. Between her and my kids, I'll have my hands full."

"I hope she recovers quickly." The significance of her statement broke through Rafe's concern. "Friday? That's three days away."

"I'm sorry for the short notice." Maryam waved a hand vaguely.

One more move for the children. One more concern for Rafe. Yet he didn't want to add to the caretaker's burden. "Can you recommend a place?"

"I have a few suggestions, but frankly..." She made a clicking noise with her tongue.

Surely she didn't anticipate trouble placing Juan just because of a little rowdiness. "Juan's behavior isn't *that* aggressive."

"I didn't mean that," she said quickly. "The problem is that most day cares like mine are filled for the summer, and attending a center with a lot of children would be hard on those two. What they really need—"

Before she could finish, a dispute erupted in the den. Rafe recognized his nephew's voice, shouting, "Give it here!"

"Hold on." Maryam ducked out. The TV set clicked on and music filled the air.

Returning, his hostess said, "I put on a sing-along. Those seem to calm Juan, and the other kids enjoy them, too."

"I know." Videos had saved Rafe's bacon more than once since he became a sudden dad.

"My point is, Juan and Sofia are still in crisis mode.

Their parents' deaths would have been horrible for them, and that's not something you recover from overnight."

"I'm aware of that. I arranged for therapy right away, you'll recall," Rafe countered.

"That helped them through the initial shock," Maryam agreed. "However, I believe they need one-on-one attention from someone who's with them all day and gets to know them intimately." She raised a hand to stop his protest. "You've done a great job, but they're about to turn five, and in the fall they enter kindergarten. That's a huge step. If they don't start school feeling secure, they could develop behavioral problems that could seriously affect their education."

Rafe's stomach clenched. He'd been afraid of something like this. "Maybe we should see the psychologist again."

"A psychologist only listens for an hour or so a week," Maryam said. "That's no substitute for parenting."

What were the options? "I can't ask my mom to look after them. She has too many responsibilities already." Eight years ago, Rafe's mother had quit her job as a nurse's aide to care for his father after a disabling construction accident. Last year, she'd also taken in Rafe's grandma, who'd suffered a heart attack when she learned of Manuel's and Cara's deaths.

"What about Brooke?" Maryam referred to Rafe's cousin Oliver's new wife. Bubbly and outgoing, she lived up the street and adored the kids.

"She's still working at the orthodontist's office," he pointed out.

"Surely she'll be taking maternity leave."

"Not until September." Brooke's baby was due the

following month. "Then I presume she'll need to adjust to her new role. Besides, that'll be too late. Your mother's coming on Friday."

As the noise level from the den rose again, Maryam sighed. "Maybe you should hire a nanny."

"A nanny?" Rafe had once joked with Oliver about employing one, but he hadn't been serious. "I doubt I could afford it."

"The Yellow Pages list several licensed registries." Maryam had apparently looked into the matter. "I have no idea what they charge. Perhaps for a few months you could manage it."

Clearly, he had to do *something*. "I'll check on that. Is Friday absolutely your last day?"

She nodded.

"That's going to be hard on them." Despite Sofia's grumbling this morning, his niece and nephew had grown accustomed to this environment.

"Our kids can play together, so there won't be a complete break. In fact, I suspect they'll enjoy being playmates a lot more when they aren't around one another all day," Maryam said.

Rafe had to accept the inevitable fact that his convenient day care arrangement was about to end. "Thanks. I appreciate all you've done this past year." She'd offered valuable advice and occasionally kept the children late when business delayed him. "Give your mother my best wishes."

"I will. Let me know how it goes."

"Will do."

He poked his nose into the den to say goodbye. While the musical video ran in the background, the girls were playing with dolls, and Juan and Luther zoomed toy cars across the floor. They barely acknowledged him, which he took as a good thing.

Despite their earlier protests, his niece and nephew really had settled in at Maryam's. Now if the wind would only change and bring Mary Poppins fluttering to his doorstep with her umbrella unfurled, Rafe would be a happy man.

In the meantime, he had a business to run.

At the garage, Mario had done his usual excellent job of performing triage on early-arriving customers. Too bad the guy didn't plan on sticking around. A tenor who studied music at nearby California State University, Fullerton, Mario dreamed of a career in opera.

Despite having sung in his own church choir while growing up, Rafe couldn't tell Puccini from…what was that other composer's name? Oh, yeah, Verdi. But he did enjoy Mario's occasional bursts of song while working.

Sending the mechanic to tune up a Volkswagen, Rafe took over the repairs on Sherry's car. The sedan carried a pleasant scent of leather and perfume, despite the beating it had endured since Winston absconded with it.

The morning flew by. Rafe took a short break at lunch to consume a peanut-butter-and-jelly sandwich and a bag of chips. He'd cut back on expenses to save money for the kids' future needs.

Now they needed a nanny. Rafe wondered what that was going to cost.

He took out the Yellow Pages and started calling. A busy signal greeted him at the first agency, while two more went to voice mail. The staff must be on lunch break, Rafe reflected, and he entered the numbers in his cell phone to try again later.

Resuming work on Sherry's car, he noted with satisfaction how much progress he and Mario had made. A couple more days and they'd be finished with the darn thing.

As he adjusted the front seat, something glittered in the newly uncovered dust. Rafe fished out a small object that shimmered in the light.

Diamonds cascaded from an earring. He'd never been much for jewelry, but these shone with stunning blue-white depths. On Sherry's earlobes, they no doubt mirrored her sparkling eyes.

Must be worth a bundle. A mere bauble for the rich divorcée she used to be. Now she'd probably prefer cash.

In the office, Rafe wrapped the earring in a clean cloth and locked it in the desk drawer. He'd return it when work on the car was done.

As he turned away, his cell phone pealed. Maryam's phone number showed on the display. "Rafe," he answered.

Her anxious tone sent a chill through him even before her words registered. "It's Juan," she said. "He's missing."

"Are you sure he isn't hiding somewhere?" Once, Juan had ducked into a closet, sending Rafe and Sofia on an impromptu and rather anxious game of hide-and-seek.

"Luther says he sneaked outside while I was fixing lunch. He isn't in the yard."

"What about the neighbors?"

She rushed on. "Minnie hasn't seen him. Grace Ching checked her yard and yours. No luck." Grace, whose eldest daughter babysat for Rafe on weekends, lived next to them. "I can't leave the kids to go canvass the neighborhood. Shall I call the police?"

Juan might flee from a stranger in uniform. If he ran far enough, he'd get lost again. A mischievous outing could turn deadly if a panicky little boy wandered into the open hills north of Harmony Circle.

"Let's not jump the gun," Rafe said. "I'll be there in a few minutes."

"Okay." Before clicking off, Maryam added, "I think I know why he got upset. Luther told him about my mother coming to live with us, and that he'll have to attend a new day care center. If I'd been aware of it, I'd have reassured him, but I didn't find out until after he vanished."

"Thanks for telling me."

Rafe hung up and explained the situation to Mario and his other mechanic, Jeb Alonzo. As an afterthought, he pocketed Sherry's earring. Since he planned to go door to door, asking his neighbors if they'd seen Juan, he might get a chance to drop it off.

Or not. Who gave a darn about diamonds, anyway? The only thing that mattered was finding Juan.

Chapter Two

For Sherry LaSalle, the most painful part of the day should have been when she emerged from her cottage to see Rafe Montoya regarding her with scorn. Dark, brooding men had never been her type, but considering that she'd married a manipulator with gorgeous silver hair and nearly wed a sunny blond con man, perhaps it was time she revised her criteria.

Anyway, she'd taken the high road by ignoring him. Or tried to. The sun glaring in her eyes had produced a grimace that he might have interpreted the wrong way.

Aside from this, the most awkward part of the day by any normal standards should have been when the head of the public relations company she used to employ told her that, sorry, she just wasn't qualified for the job opening.

As a receptionist.

During Sherry's seven-year marriage to Elliott LaSalle, the attorney who'd handled her parents' estate and offered emotional support after their deaths in a boating accident, she used to have a social secretary. Now she wasn't even competent enough to *be* one. She had only one semester of college, no computer skills and no accounting experience. Her father, an entrepreneur, and her mother, a former beauty queen, had died before Sherry had decided on a career.

Until recently, that hadn't been a problem. Even when she faced poverty, she'd considered the situation temporary.

With her extensive experience organizing charity events, she'd assumed she could get hired as a party planner or public relations spokesperson. Wrong on both counts. Her inquiries had met rejection at every turn.

Before the media dropped her as old news, they'd crowed that Orange County's golden girl might have to do honest work for a change. Since when was being a wife and philanthropist not honest work? And how exactly did a woman with absolutely no wage-earning credentials persuade employers of her worth?

So far no one was willing to give her a chance. But failing again to land a job hadn't been the worst part of the day.

Nor was she totally dismayed by the bills piling up on the delicate mahogany desk in her living room, although Sherry did find them worrisome. Her lawyer had called her foolish for giving her remaining funds to the employees that Winston—she still thought of him by that name, although it had been a fraud—had left in the lurch, but how could she refuse to help? She'd gladly donated a few thousand dollars each to his secretary, a single mom, and his earnest young accountant. Surely they needed the money more than she did.

The rest of her funds had dwindled with shocking speed. Bills kept pouring in, including ones for clothes and luxury items Winston had charged on Sherry's cards.

Except for a small amount the lawyer had insisted she set aside for taxes, she owned nothing but this house and the furnishings inherited from her parents. The lawyer was gone now, too, his bills collecting dust in her stack.

Still, the worst, blackest moment didn't arrive until after Sherry finished picking at the salad she'd made for lunch. That was when she summoned the courage to open the newspaper to the society page.

She used to relish scanning the lovely photos of a fund-raising ball or dinner, enjoying the images of her friends dressed in their best designer gowns. The men looked so noble in their tuxedos, like modern-day princes.

Now she gazed hungrily at the participants at the ball that had followed an opening night at the opera. Longing twisted through Sherry as she spotted Becky Rosen, wife of software magnate Abe Rosen, in the midst of a group. What a great friend she used to be, before Sherry's divorce forced her and her husband to choose sides. They'd chosen Elliott because he was Abe's golfing buddy.

Sherry felt even worse when she spotted cool, regal Helen Salonica dominating a scene from the gathering. Helen and her orthodontist husband, Nicholas, had helped Sherry through the split and had stood beside her and Winston at society functions.

Then Winston had stolen a hundred fifty thousand dollars from the couple. They'd narrowly escaped getting scalped for an additional million, coming within inches of losing their home and business.

Helen would never forgive Sherry. Neither would the other friends who'd followed her lead and trusted Winston with their money.

Everyone had assumed that Sherry had at least visited the Caribbean resort he claimed to be building. She hadn't. She'd believed the lies on Winston's splendid Web site and glossy résumé.

Rather than being a graduate of Harvard Business School and the son of New York industrialists, he was a junior-college dropout whose politician father had been convicted of taking bribes. Winston hadn't been a financial consultant and real estate developer, either, as he'd claimed. Instead, he had a history of scamming people and staying one step ahead of the law, changing his identity to avoid detection.

During the turmoil after her husband, Elliott, abandoned her for a twenty-two-year-old journalism student, she'd met Winston at a party. Handsome and sympathetic, he'd dazzled her with the names of several famous people he'd described as financial clients and, before she knew it, was guiding her through what had felt like an overwhelming maze of decisions. At Winston's urging, he'd requested her alimony in a lump sum so she could invest it. Or, as she now realized, so he could steal it.

The only hope of redemption lay with the FBI agents pursuing Winston and the stolen money. Yet sometimes Sherry still didn't believe the man she'd thought she loved would do such a vile thing. In weak moments, she missed his thick blond hair, his engaging smile and his take-charge manner.

No. She refused to be manipulated ever again, or to abandon her independence to fit into some guy's way of living.

Sherry intended to stand on her own feet, wobbling

a bit on her high heels but independent nonetheless. Okay, at the moment she was flat broke and without job prospects, but that would pass. She hadn't run out of jobs to apply for—in fact, she'd scheduled an appointment for later this afternoon.

Considering that she'd never balanced a checkbook until a month ago, she figured she deserved *some* credit. If nobody else intended to give her a break, she'd give herself one.

Setting the paper aside, she reached down from the sofa for her guitar case. Music always helped restore her peace of mind. After Winston's abrupt departure without so much as a goodbye, she'd run through almost everything Rodgers and Hammerstein ever wrote. When the clamor of his victims and the press threatened to drown her in a flood of outrage, she'd undertaken the challenging melodies of Andrew Lloyd Webber. There was nothing like *The Phantom of the Opera* to restore one's mood.

Singing had been Sherry's favorite activity in high school. She'd fantasized about a career in music, but a voice teacher finally told her the truth—she sang well enough for amateur musicals, period.

After that, she'd quit singing entirely until Becky Rosen, who'd studied voice seriously before her marriage, encouraged Sherry to join in duets at fund-raising galas. Sherry shook her head. If she thought any more about how much she missed Becky, her throat would clog.

Sherry tuned the strings, then looped the guitar strap across her shoulder and launched into "The Sound of Music." As her voice swelled, her spirits lifted. The cramped living room seemed to expand, and, reflected in an ornate framed mirror, her mother's floral-patterned fabrics and china vases brought back memories of her happy childhood.

Through the window, Sherry noted that the sun had emerged to highlight the oranges and purples of a bird of paradise plant in the front garden. She'd grown to love the simplicity of her cottage with its hand-carved shutters, sprawling porch and old-fashioned plantings. No wonder the neighbors had campaigned to save it. At least one good thing had come of losing her money.

She was transitioning into "Do-Re-Mi" when a movement outside caught her eye. Was that a clump of dark hair bobbing along the porch and ducking beneath the open window?

A child. Listening.

Amused, Sherry ran through the lilting tune. When she segued to "My Favorite Things," she heard a sigh.

Easing to her feet, she strolled toward the door without interrupting her cadence. She didn't want to scare the little person, but it touched her that someone else appreciated music. Maybe that someone else felt lonely, too.

Like her.

Holding the last note of the song, she eased open the door. She caught one glimpse of a startled face, and then a boy sprang from beneath the window.

In his alarm, he ran right into her. Thank goodness she'd kicked off her heels, or she'd have collapsed in a heap of guitar strings and splintered wood.

Instead, while stumbling backward, Sherry managed to lift her instrument out of harm's way and scoop a protective arm around the child. Rather than falling, they both staggered about the porch as they fought for balance.

At last, breathless, they broke apart. "Wow," Sherry said before her visitor could bolt. "You're a terrific dancer."

"I am?" Those dark eyes, that stocky, defiant stance… She recognized him as Rafe's nephew, of course. Her real estate agent, Oliver Armstrong, had explained about his cousin's decision to adopt the orphaned twins, which meant her neighbor couldn't be a *complete* ogre.

Besides, how could anyone resist this cutie?

"That was the best waltz I ever had on a front porch," she told him.

The boy wiggled as if itching to run, but stood his ground. "Are you really a witch?"

Sherry stifled a laugh at his boldness. No question where *that* suspicion originated. "I've heard of singing nuns, but never a singing witch. What's your name?"

"Juan."

"I'm Sherry." Gravely, she shook hands, and found his small and warm.

She wished she knew more about kids. Elliott's sons had been teenagers when she wed their father, and they'd chosen to ignore her entirely. Although she'd hoped to bear her own babies, her husband had kept delaying, and finally dumped her.

"If you like my singing, you can come inside and join me," she told the little boy.

He considered. "Do you have cookies?"

"I suppose I must. Witches are famous for serving gingerbread." At least that's what she'd believed as a child, based on the story of Hansel and Gretel.

"What's gingerbread?"

The poor, deprived kid! "It's delicious," she said. "My mom used to build gingerbread houses at Christmas, with candy canes along the walls and icing on the roof. They were almost too pretty to eat." Three years ago, Sherry had taught the skill to Becky, and together they'd created an entire gingerbread village to auction for charity.

Three years ago now seemed like three centuries.

"Will you make me a house?" Juan asked.

"I'm afraid that takes hours and hours."

His face fell. She hated disappointing him. "We could bake gingerbread men," Sherry offered.

"Can we eat them?"

"Sure. They're cookies, only they're shaped like little people."

"Cool!"

Sherry ushered Juan inside. In addition to finding him adorable, she was glad for the company. Her only guest since moving in had been Minnie from next door, whose late sister used to own this house. As executor of her will, Minnie had sold it to Sherry. Even then, she'd only stopped by out of curiosity.

There hadn't been a lot of guests at the luxury apartment Sherry and Winston had shared in the year since her divorce, either. Still, she'd raided gourmet shops for kitchen gear, and now she had someone to bake for.

Inside, Juan's gaze fixed on the china hutch. "My mom has dishes like that. They're pretty."

Sherry hadn't expected him to appreciate porcelain. "The characters painted on them come from fairy tales. Cinderella's my favorite. What about yours?"

"I used to have a cup with Peter Rabbit on it." His voice thickened. "It got burned up."

With a jolt, she recalled hearing that his parents had

died in a fire. How terrible. "I'm sorry, Juan. Why don't we get started on those gingerbread men?" She steered the boy into the kitchen. "First we'd better wash our hands."

"Yeah." Even on tiptoe he was too short for the sink, so she hauled over a chair. Standing behind him, she made sure he did a thorough job. After he jumped down, she scrubbed her hands, too.

"Now we're set, except for aprons." She retrieved a blue-and-white check for him, red-and-white for herself.

While the oven preheated, they stirred the ingredients in a large bowl. Quite a bit of dough found its way into Juan's mouth, but there was plenty left to roll out on wax paper.

Sherry brought out a man-shaped cookie cutter and sprayed it lightly with oil to prevent the dough from sticking. "First time I've used this. Ever cut cookies before?"

"I made Big Bird out of clay." Taking the cutter, he pressed it into the dough. His hand jerked, mushing the shape. "Uh-oh."

"No problem." Sherry rolled out the dough again. "We get do-overs. See?"

"Cool!" Clearly it was his favorite adjective.

"You have to be gentle with gingerbread people." She demonstrated how to lift the cutter without bringing the dough with it.

Frowning in concentration, the boy imitated her movements. The result: a perfect miniature man, if you didn't count the slightly bent arm.

"Good job," Sherry said. "How about raisins for the eyes?"

"Can I put them in?"

"Sure."

After a few cross-eyed gingerbread men, he got the hang of the decorations. Soon they were tucking two full cookie sheets into the oven.

"You're not really a witch, are you?" Juan said.

"Nope. Disappointed?" Sherry set the timer.

"'Course not. A real witch might push me in the oven."

"I wouldn't!" Sherry noticed his grin. "You're kidding."

"Gotcha." He beamed. "I can tell you're a good witch."

Why was he so fixated on witches? "Did you come here for a special reason?" she asked.

He took a breath. "So you can do a spell."

That explained a lot. "What kind of spell?"

"To bring my mom and dad back," he said softly.

Tears pricked her eyes. "Nobody on earth has that kind of power, Juan. If I could do that, I'd bring my parents back, too."

He folded his arms. "What happened to them?"

She wondered if talking about death with a kid would give him nightmares. Well, it was a bit late to worry about that, Sherry decided. "They were sailing when another boat knocked them into the water."

"They couldn't swim?"

"Yes, but they were too hurt. It happened so fast, nobody had time to save them." Enough about that. The look on Juan's face told her she needed to lighten the mood, and she had an idea. "Do you know 'Row, Row, Row Your Boat'?"

"Sure. Sort of."

"Let's have a go. When we're done, we'll have something to drink." She led him to the couch.

Juan curled against her as she lifted the guitar. Sherry

loved the weight of his small body against her and the trusting expression in those large eyes. How different it was from the way his uncle glared at her. She wondered if Rafe warmed to anyone.

Of course he must. Just not to her.

She strummed a few chords and began the simple song. Juan's sweet soprano joined hers after a few bars.

Contentment spread through Sherry as their voices blended. She hadn't felt this close to anyone for a long while. She wished Juan could come visit every day, but his uncle might object. Besides, she was going to get a job, and the sooner the better.

For right now, though, she loved having him here.

JUAN HADN'T TURNED UP by the time Rafe arrived in Harmony Circle. He launched his search at the vacant house past Maryam's, scanning the yard for movement and calling the boy's name. An empty house could become what the police called an attractive nuisance, tempting kids to break in, but this one appeared intact. The owners had moved out of state and refused to rent it in case their adult daughter ever decided to live here. In the meantime, they'd arranged for their neighbor, gardener Bart Ryan, to tend the yard.

Bart wasn't home, either, nor were most residents of that prong of the horseshoe. The only person Rafe encountered was Diane Lorenz, a schoolteacher who had the summer off. She volunteered to search the far stretch, which left the curved central section to Rafe—including the cottage he'd hoped to avoid.

He doubted Sherry LaSalle had any desire to see him on her doorstep; however, he had to be thorough.

As he approached, the smell of gingerbread floated through the air. Despite its sweetness, Rafe felt an immediate, visceral anger as the scent tugged him back to an evening more than a decade earlier, shortly before Christmas. He'd been a senior in high school, working as a valet at a fancy restaurant. That night he'd been kept busy, thanks to a private party. He could smell gingerbread in the air, reminding him of the *marranitos* molasses cookies his grandmother used to cut into little pig shapes.

As Rafe accepted the car keys from late-arriving guests, a blond girl in a cranberry velvet dress had darted out of the restaurant to greet them. The sight of her merry blue eyes and animated face had filled him with the sudden belief that they knew each other, or were meant to know each other. If she would only notice him, he'd thought, she would surely feel the same.

Then her gaze had flicked across him and away without so much as a smile, as if he were no more than a part of the scenery. He'd felt dismissed and disrespected.

Clearly this rich girl disdained a mere Hispanic boy who parked cars. Sherry Parker—an arriving guest had called out her name—had been saving her precious self for a multimillionaire like Elliott LaSalle, the rich-as-Midas attorney she'd married a few years later.

Grumpily, Rafe strode toward the cottage. As he drew closer, he heard voices join in a rendition of "Row, Row, Row Your Boat."

He recognized his nephew's youthful soprano. Juan was safe! Thank heaven.

But Rafe wasn't pleased to discover that Ms. High and Mighty was having fun at the expense of those she must realize were searching for the child. Living in relative poverty still hadn't taught her common courtesy, Rafe reflected as he rang the bell.

For the sake of peace in the neighborhood, Rafe tried to calm his anger. If possible, he'd like to reclaim his nephew without setting off fireworks. But holding his temper had never been Rafe's strong suit.

Chapter Three

The oven timer rang at the same moment the door chimed. Sherry set down her guitar. “Scoot, sweetie,” she told Juan, who seemed in danger of toppling if she got up too fast.

“Okay.” He sank against the cushions.

Making a split-second choice, Sherry threw open the front door first. The sight of her neighbor’s stern face startled her. “Gotta get the cookies,” she said before padding into the kitchen.

Even with her back turned, she could feel Rafe glowering as she snatched the pot holders and removed the trays from the oven. How could anyone nurse a bad mood in a house fragrant with gingerbread?

The man ought to appreciate her entertaining his nephew. He shouldn’t let such a young child run around unsupervised, anyway, although Sherry didn’t choose to tell him so.

She set the cookies on the stove to cool, removed the whistling kettle from the burner and returned to see Juan fling himself into his uncle’s arms. The notion of being dropped clearly didn’t enter the boy’s mind. He simply leaped, and Rafe caught him, swung him around and held him tight. Dark hair pressed against dark hair, as if they were burrowing into each other.

The man's solid, protective form dominated her living room. Despite her reservations, Sherry enjoyed the sight of that well-muscled body in the blue mechanic's jumpsuit. If she didn't know Rafe for a thoroughgoing grouch, she'd consider him the sort of man a woman could lean on.

Not her, though. Sherry was finished relying on men.

"Thanks for…watching him," Rafe said gruffly. "See you later."

"You're leaving?" she asked.

"That's the idea."

Juan stared at his uncle in horror. "No."

"Sorry, sprite."

"But he has to eat the gingerbread men. He helped make them." To her the logic seemed irrefutable.

Clearly unwilling to place his hopes in her debating ability, Juan slithered out of his uncle's grasp and raced for the kitchen. "They're mine!"

"Juan!" Rafe shouted.

How could a child move that fast? "Stop! They're hot, sweetie." Sherry rounded the corner to see a tiny hand halt in midair, inches from a metal tray.

"Oh." Juan tucked his arm quickly behind him.

She hugged the little boy. "You could have been burned."

Rafe halted behind her. "He's like a tornado in human form."

As she released the child, Sherry tried to ignore a delicious sensitivity tingling up her spine. The man might be tall, powerful and protective, but he was only here because of his nephew.

She dug a spatula out of a drawer. "Let's give those cookies a minute to cool and then we'll eat. Please join us," she told her neighbor. "There's plenty."

Rafe acquiesced with a short nod. "They smell great. My grandmother used to bake gingerbread cookies shaped like pigs. They're called *marranitos.*"

"Pigs? That's a new one on me." She loved the notion. "What a great idea."

"Can I take some home for my sister?" Juan asked.

Sherry ruffled his hair. "Of course. How considerate."

"And extras for me?"

"Ah, a method to your madness," she joked. "Sure."

"Juan, don't be greedy," his uncle cautioned.

"Just one extra for me," the boy corrected.

At this quick but self-serving recovery, the corners of Rafe's mouth twitched, revealing dents in his cheeks. He wasn't such a grouch, after all, Sherry thought. And he obviously doted on his nephew.

As she poured hot water over orange-spice bags in a teapot, she saw Rafe's gaze sweep the polished cabinets, the sprigged china canisters and, on the wall, a framed needlepoint picture of a small girl in a garden. "You have old-fashioned taste," he observed with what sounded like approval.

"Most of these things were my mother's. I kept them in storage during my marriage. Elliott insisted on having a designer decorate our place, but I never really liked that spare, half-empty look." She didn't know why she'd confided that except that she'd had hardly anyone to talk to for weeks.

"I'd have expected you to appreciate this cottage more," Rafe said. "Most of us consider it a piece of Brea's history."

Did he *have* to dwell on that sore point? "I'm over that whole business. You should be, too."

"Point taken." He didn't seem offended, though. "Anything I can do to help?"

"If you don't mind grabbing some plates for the cookies, that would be great." Sherry opened a cabinet to reveal her everyday china.

"I'll get right on it."

"Uncle Rafe! Wash your hands." After a startled pause, Juan added, "Please."

Chuckling, the man went to the sink. "It appears your good manners have rubbed off on my nephew."

"Oh, Juan has good manners. He simply forgets to use them sometimes," Sherry said. "Now, let's put these cookies on a platter."

As she and the boy transferred the gingerbread men, Rafe's attention settled on her like a warm blanket. She was almost disappointed when he began distributing the silverware.

"Oh, I nearly forgot." After setting down the last spoon, he picked up his cell phone. "I found him," he told whoever answered. "He's fine. We'll be there in a few minutes."

He must be calling the day care lady, Sherry mused. "Juan wasn't supposed to be out playing?"

"No." Rafe pressed a second button. "Diane? You can call off the hunt. He was at Mrs. LaSalle's. Thanks for the help."

The whole neighborhood had been out canvassing? Sherry blushed. "I'm sorry. It never occurred to me that people might be searching for him. I seem to have a talent for causing trouble."

"Juan's safe, and that's all that matters."

Perhaps sensing that his uncle was upset, Juan picked up the platter of cookies and teetered across the floor with it. "I'm hungry."

Sherry's instinct was to grab the fragile plate. Instead, she bit her lip and let him try. All went well until the last moment, when Juan staggered against the table, rattling the china and her nerves.

Rafe hoisted the platter to safety, moving with remarkable grace. Replacing spark plugs and adjusting carburetors probably took a lot of dexterity, Sherry reflected. Also, although she'd never considered it before, owning a garage meant dealing with customer service and business finance. She hadn't given Rafe enough credit.

There were new lessons to be learned every day. Including the fact that supervising a small boy involved constant vigilance.

"Juan has trouble obeying rules," Rafe advised as he pulled out a chair for each of them. "Such as sneaking out of the babysitter's house, or asking permission before he lifts breakable objects."

"I'm sorry," Juan said.

"He's only—how old? Six?" Sherry asked.

"Four."

Well, that explained the search. "Napkins on laps," she ordered.

Uncle and nephew paused guiltily, set down the cookies they'd grabbed and complied. Score a point for her side.

Sharing an impromptu tea party with Rafe Montoya might not be the best idea she'd ever had, Sherry decided. It was like inviting a bear into your hot tub. A sophisticated bear with tantalizing dark eyes.

It was too late to change her mind, though. Besides, she'd never forget the blissful expressions on the Montoyas' faces as they tasted their gingerbread men.

She would bake every day for a reward like that.

WHO'D HAVE FIGURED the society princess could cook, and keep her household spotless without an army of servants? Sherry had been kind to Juan, too. Moreover, she appeared to be a strong-minded lady in the best sense of the word, not arrogant but assertive. Rafe admired that quality in people.

With strands of blond hair curling free of their pins, and an errant dab of flour on one cheek, she bore little resemblance to the frosty society debutante he'd met before. At some level he recognized a tug of attraction, but it was a bad idea. Aside from their previous disagreements, he harbored no illusions as to what the future held.

Sherry belonged to a different world, and sooner or later she'd return to it. A world that he could never join and didn't wish to. For now, however, he was glad to establish a sort of truce.

"Do you wander off by yourself much?" she asked Juan.

He finished chewing. "No. I came to see you."

That surprised Rafe. "Why?"

Sherry answered for him. "He believed I was a witch. Where do you suppose he got that notion?" She gave him a sideways glance that spoke volumes.

Rafe choked on a mouthful of crumbs. He'd never figured Sherry would learn how he'd referred to her. To add to his embarrassment, the crumbs went down the wrong way, making him cough until his throat was raw.

She whacked him on the shoulder, hard enough to rattle his spinal column and probably reshape his kidneys. Rafe gulped his tea before she could try it again. He couldn't blame her, though.

"He asked me to work a spell to bring back his parents," she explained.

"Oh." The childlike logic of that notion squeezed Rafe's heart.

"Could a real witch do that?" Juan asked.

"No," Sherry told him solemnly. "But your parents already *are* with you. Their love is all around like a big happy cloud. I'll bet they're glad you're with your uncle Rafe and that you've learned to bake gingerbread men."

The boy stared at his plate. "I hear my mom singing to me sometimes." A smile broke through. "Like you did."

Rafe hadn't seen his nephew connect with anyone this openly in all the months they'd spent together. How amazing that the boy had chosen Sherry LaSalle.

Abruptly, he recalled the earring in his pocket. "I found something of yours, by the way." He produced the cloth.

Unwrapped, the diamonds gleamed in the afternoon light. Sherry inhaled sharply. "Thank goodness. I was so upset."

"Pretty," Juan announced.

She reached for the earring with a reverent air. "I couldn't imagine where I lost this. My parents gave me these not long before they died." That explained the emotional reaction. "I was going to refashion its mate into a pendant, but this is much better. Thank you."

"You're welcome."

While she put the earring away, Rafe and Juan cleared the table. On Sherry's return, she wrapped the extra cookies in wax paper.

"Keep a few for yourself," Rafe advised.

"I don't need the calories. Juan can share them with his day care friends." She tucked the package into an orange-and-black gift bag. "Appropriate colors for a witch, don't you think?"

The last of Rafe's resentment dissipated. Okay, she'd tried to remake the neighborhood to suit her overblown tastes, but today he'd seen a much better side of Sherry. Perhaps that sunny air she projected wasn't entirely an illusion.

"I'm willing to let bygones be bygones," he said. "How about you?"

"Gladly." Her blue eyes shone as she held out the bag. When he took it and their hands touched, Rafe enjoyed the contact more than he should have.

Something beeped. Fumbling beneath her apron, Sherry withdrew an organizer from her pocket. "Oh my gosh! I have a job interview in half an hour. I completely forgot, and I'm a mess!"

Rafe checked the impulse to point out that her free-falling hair and skewed dress were sexy. "Nothing you can't fix. We'll get out of your way."

"Drop in anytime." The invitation seemed to include him along with Juan.

"Thanks." Grateful that his nephew didn't throw a tantrum about leaving, Rafe escorted him outside. When he glanced back at the cottage, he half expected to see it glimmering with fairy dust.

Rafe's life hadn't exactly been full of delightful surprises. How doubly astonishing to find one right across the street, even though it probably wouldn't last.

At the day care, Maryam greeted Rafe with relief. "I've never had a child run away before."

"I didn't run away. I went to see the princess." Juan darted off to join his playmates.

He'd stopped referring to their neighbor as a witch, Rafe noted. "Sherry LaSalle taught him to bake gingerbread men. It never occurred to her we'd be searching for him." Producing the cookies, Rafe explained about the boy's hope of getting his mother and father restored by magic. "I should be more careful what I say around him. Calling her a witch wasn't very discreet, either."

"No matter how careful you are, kids pick up the strangest ideas from TV or elsewhere." Maryam sniffed the cookies appreciatively. "How nice of our new neighbor to send refreshments. I didn't picture her as the homey type."

"Neither did I."

He took his leave and was getting in his car when he heard a female voice calling his name. Puzzled, Rafe scanned the area until he spotted Sherry in front of her house, waving anxiously.

If she exerted herself any further, the hair she'd smoothed into place was likely to tumble down again, and he half hoped it would. She did seem genuinely distressed, and Rafe hurried over. "What's wrong?"

Sherry pointed to the car in her driveway, which was tilted ominously. "When I backed out of the garage, something felt wrong."

"Two flat tires on the same side. That's unusual." Crouching, he spotted jagged puncture marks in each. "How did this happen?"

Sherry clasped her hands together. “There’s some construction happening around the corner from Friendship Lane. I must have hit a few nails or something.”

“We’ll have to tow it to the shop.” She didn’t carry two spares, he knew, since this was his loaner car.

“I’m already running late. I’ll call a cab.” She took out her phone. “Oh, dear. Cabs take forever, don’t they? I’d better postpone the appointment.”

“Sounds like a good idea.”

She wavered. “That’s going to make me look unreliable, isn’t it? I never do things like this. Usually I’m organized.” Judging by the tremor in her voice, she seemed on the verge of a meltdown. “I already lost one job this morning. I mean, the possibility of a job. I can’t afford to lose another over something like this.”

Rafe straightened. “How far is this place you’re going?”

“About ten minutes away.”

“I could drop you off.” What kind of jerk would leave his neighbor stranded? Besides, he was curious to see where she’d applied.

Sherry gazed at him gratefully. “I can’t believe you’re being this generous, after the way I treated you. I’d be happy to babysit whenever you need me, to repay the favor.”

“Sure, if I get in a jam,” Rafe agreed. “Let’s go.” He set off for his car, with her scurrying to keep up.

He opened the passenger door, and watched in amusement as dainty Sherry LaSalle slid her silk-clad rear onto the rough seat of the rebuilt cruiser. He’d bought it cheap at a police auction, repainted it and outfitted the old clunker with civilian-friendly equipment.

She stared around the blue interior. "This reminds me of a…"

"Cop car?"

"I wasn't sure I should say that."

"It *is* a cop car." He switched on the powerful engine. "Or used to be."

She cleared her throat. "Do, um, do most mechanics drive cop cars?"

Rafe laughed. "Only if they get a terrific deal at an auction."

She settled against the seat back. "I must sound awfully ignorant."

"Nothing wrong with a little naiveté." In Rafe's younger days, he'd have roared forward to demonstrate the car's horsepower. Since adopting kids, however, he'd become more cautious, even when there wasn't a pedestrian in sight. "Mind giving directions?"

"Turn right at the corner, then left at the next…" She reddened. "You didn't mean that specific, did you? Go to Imperial Highway and head east."

"Will do."

They drove for a few minutes in edgy silence. Despite today's accord, people who'd fought bitter public battles didn't recover from them in an instant, Rafe mused.

Sherry must have been thinking along the same lines. "I'm sorry you and I got off on the wrong foot when I bought the cottage," she said. "We met under unfortunate circumstances."

Her airy perfume filled the car. Thanks to its influence, Rafe blurted something he hadn't meant to confide. "We had an encounter before this, although I doubt you'd remember it."

"We did?"

"It would have been, oh, fourteen years ago." Strange that he recalled the details so clearly. "December of my senior year in high school. I used to park cars for a restaurant in L.A. Your family was hosting a party, and you came out to greet friends. You wore this dark red dress and had your hair curled."

"You remember what I wore? That's amazing," she said. "Did we talk?"

"No."

"Did I step on your foot or something?"

Rafe laughed. "That isn't why I noticed you." He could hardly explain that he'd felt a connection when their eyes met. In retrospect, the notion seemed juvenile. "You looked remarkably pretty."

"Thanks." Nostalgia warmed her expression. "That must have been my thirteenth birthday party."

"You were thirteen? You looked older." No wonder she hadn't flirted with him. Now that she pointed it out, Rafe did realize there was a four-year gap in their ages. He simply hadn't added things up.

"You thought I was ignoring you?" Sherry asked. "Honestly, I must have stomped on people's feelings all my life and been completely oblivious."

"It's not your fault." Rafe wasn't sure why he'd reacted strongly to the situation, except that over the years he'd taken a lot of snubs from people like her. Or like he'd assumed she was. "You were quite a fox for thirteen."

She smiled. "I'm sure you were gorgeous, especially if you wore some sort of uniform, but way out of my league, age-wise. Go straight," she added as they approached an intersection.

"Will do."

They drove through Brea's redeveloped downtown, with its stylish restaurants and shops, and continued east past the mall, the freeway and assorted office buildings. Rafe's curiosity grew. "Where is your job interview?"

"Just a store."

"A retail store?"

"Is there another kind?"

"Guess not." He'd expected her to seek a white-collar job. Perhaps she preferred to work at an exclusive boutique, although this was hardly the sort of area for that.

"Turn left here." She indicated the parking lot of a large discount store.

"This is it?" He couldn't disguise his disbelief.

She wrinkled her nose. "I used to call it Bottom-of-the-Barrel Mart. Ironic, huh? Well, maybe not. I *am* scraping the bottom of my barrel."

"They pay only minimum wage." This woman probably spent more on her annual wardrobe than his garage earned.

"Being a former socialite isn't much of a job qualification, I've discovered." Sherry shrugged. "Maybe someday the government will catch Winston and get my money back, but in the meantime the bills are piling up. I have to start somewhere."

"None of your friends offered you a job?" In Rafe's circles, people helped their pals.

"After I encouraged them to throw their money down a sinkhole? Most of them won't even return my phone calls."

"What about an employment agency?" That seemed a better move than applying to places willy-nilly.

"I tried. I'm not sure which was worse, the counselor who returned my résumé and told me I should finish college, or the lady who turned out to be friends with the first Mrs. LaSalle. Her comments bordered on spiteful."

That *was* a discouraging story. "You figure this is the best you can do?"

Sherry stared at the broad storefront. "I took the aptitude test online, so they practically *have* to hire me, right? I just wish I'd remembered to stop by earlier and scope out the place like I planned, but I intend to become an expert on cut-rate appliances and tablecloths and… What else do they sell? Oh, right. Toys and gardening equipment. I *did* review the Web site."

Her can-do attitude impressed him. "I'll wait for you." An interview shouldn't take long, not when she'd already completed the test.

"I'll catch a bus home," Sherry protested. "You've done more than enough already."

"The bus stops half a mile from our houses, and you're wearing heels. Plus I doubt you brought a schedule with you."

"They run on a schedule?"

He couldn't leave this babe in the woods to find her way home. "I'll stick around."

She opened the car door. "I already owe you more than I can repay. There's no need, truly." With a twinkle of a grin, she was gone.

The car felt empty. *What a bright spirit,* Rafe thought, and pulled into a parking space. Regardless of Sherry's instructions, he intended to hang around and find out how she fared.

Chapter Four

The huge interior of the discount store, with its noise and crowds, nearly overwhelmed Sherry. She yearned to run outside, flag down Rafe and beg him to take her home.

She grabbed the handle of a shopping cart for support. *You have to do this. No chickening out.*

Besides, she'd resolved never again to depend on a guy. Even one as amazingly considerate as Rafe.

He'd offered help when he had every reason to resent her. On top of that, she'd worried him by taking in Juan without considering that someone might be searching for him. She'd also flattened the tires on the car she'd forced Rafe to loan her while he repaired her sedan for free. Deep inside she knew perfectly well it was unfair to hold him responsible for Winston's theft—Rafe was just as much a victim of Winston's scheming as she was—but she'd let the lawyer talk her into it.

And Rafe had returned her earring. A lesser man might have believed himself justified in selling it as compensation for his labor.

Okay, so her neighbor was practically a saint. All the

more reason for a weak-willed woman to keep her distance.

A loudspeaker announcement jolted Sherry from her reverie. The store was having a special on bras in aisle 3. Who would buy lingerie here?

I might. If I could afford it.

She needed money. Not pride, not second thoughts and not, fortunately, underwear.

Sucking up her courage, Sherry asked directions to the manager's office from a harried young woman in a rainbow-colored apron. The clerk directed her to an office at the rear of the store.

En route, Sherry wove between carts and around displays. She'd never seen such cluttered pathways or high industrial ceilings. The stores where she usually shopped had wide aisles, quiet music and velvety displays. Nevertheless, the merchandise appeared to be good quality and she recognized several of the brand names.

Finally reaching the back of the store, she burst into the office area and halted in dismay. On a row of plastic chairs sat five, no, six people, apparently waiting to interview for the same job that she wanted.

"Are you all here for job interviews?" she asked.

Heads bobbed.

Deflated, Sherry took the end seat. She'd thought only in terms of filling the requirements for the job and pleasing the assistant manager. It hadn't occurred to her that she'd be competing with so many applicants.

She recalled uneasily how, last spring, she'd scolded Brooke, the receptionist for an orthodontist who also happened to be the husband of Sherry's friend Helen. When Brooke denied rumors that she and Nicholas

Salonica were having an affair, Sherry had told her that she should quit anyway and find a new job. Sherry could still see the annoyance on Brooke's face at her high-handed assumption that changing jobs was easy.

She'd been wrong about a lot of things.

Instead of running off with her boss, Brooke had married Oliver Armstrong, the area's leading real estate broker. He also happened to be Rafe's cousin. Sherry shuddered at the prospect of running into her, which was bound to happen, since they lived right around the corner.

These past two months, she'd avoided her fellow residents, whom she assumed despised her, with good reason. She'd insulted them en masse at a meeting of the home-owners' association, referring to their houses as tiny and calling her neighbors small-minded for opposing her plan to build a mansion. Now that the dust had settled, she suspected she was going to have to eat a lot of crow.

That ought to cut down on the grocery bills, Sherry reflected dryly.

Absorbed in her musings, she didn't notice anything amiss until a woman's voice blared, "Aren't you that heiress?"

Sherry glanced around, hoping to spot an elegant woman in designer clothing who fit that description. Nope, the woman meant *her.* Normally Sherry prided herself on quick thinking, but the best response that came to her was a pathetic, "Who, me?"

"She's Sherry LaSalle," confirmed a man with a prominent paunch. "Seen her picture in the paper."

A heavyset woman in a gray sweat suit surveyed

Sherry disapprovingly. "You serious about working here? That's a mighty fancy dress."

"This?" Sherry had chosen her favorite color, pink, and her favorite designer to boost her confidence. Hadn't this woman ever heard of dressing for success?

"What're you doing here, anyway?" the large woman demanded.

"Who cares?" A stringy-haired girl in jeans and a low-cut top whipped out her cell phone. "This is the coolest thing that's happened all week. Can I take my picture with you?"

Thankful to find an admirer, Sherry agreed. The girl sat beside her, extended an arm and pressed a button. After checking the results on the view screen, she said, "Hold my seat. I gotta tell my friends!" and raced out.

"Can I have your autograph? Like, on a check?" cracked a young man.

"She's pulling a stunt," scoffed the sweat-suit lady. "Probably starring in a reality show."

Sherry's attorney had actually proposed that she seek a producer for such a show. "Audiences love to watch an heiress fall on her face," he'd said before it dawned on him how insulting the idea was.

Now, in front of an audience that apparently felt exactly that way, she strove for calm. It wasn't easy, with their stares making her feel like an escaped orangutan. "I'm applying for a job like everyone else."

"'Cause that man stole your billions?" whooped her tormentor. "People like you always have plenty stashed away."

"Honestly, I don't. And they weren't billions."

Seeing the skepticism and doubt on her tormenters'

faces, she longed for the excited girl's return. Sometimes, Sherry discovered a few minutes later, wishes came true, but not necessarily in a good way.

The young woman came back, accompanied by a bevy of giggling friends who insisted on posing with "that famous heiress." Snapshots captured Sherry half-hidden behind one girl's bushy hairdo, and grasped in a bear hug by a Goth girl with black hair and purple nails. Sherry had no doubt the images would soon be posted on the Internet.

She still didn't understand the glee with which newspapers, radio and TV stations had covered her contentious divorce. They'd packed the courtroom, thrust microphones in her face when she emerged—despite her attempts to avoid them—and painted Sherry, rather than her unfaithful husband, as the villain for demanding seven million dollars in alimony, one for every year of her childless marriage.

More shoppers drifted to the waiting area. "It *is* her."

"What's she doing here?"

"Interviewing for a job?"

They thrust out crumpled receipts and shopping lists for Sherry to autograph. She did her best to oblige, even though the muscles in her hand cramped after a few minutes.

The women, and a few men, peppered Sherry with questions. Many of the inquiries were merely curious, and a few sympathetic, but others she found offensive. Especially "Is that Winston fella good in bed?" and "Is it true you're pregnant?"

Her patience snapped. "Don't be ridiculous. I am *not* pregnant, and my ex-fiancé's libido is nobody's business!"

"Mommy, what's a libido?" asked a tyke.

"A beach house," her mother replied. "Like a cabana."

The inner office door swung open. Out ducked a young man with a bad complexion, who scurried into the crowd as if he couldn't leave fast enough. An unsuccessful job candidate, Sherry gathered.

In his wake appeared a hard-faced woman. Mrs. Fordyce, presumably. "What's happening here?"

"That's Sherry LaSalle," trumpeted one woman in a migraine-inducing voice. "The heiress. Hunting for a job, if you can believe it!"

The gingerbread men in Sherry's stomach hardened into cement. What did that woman have against her?

"Are you the applicant who gave her name as Sherry *Parker?*" The assistant manager's tone implied that she'd committed a capital crime.

"That's my maiden name." Sherry struggled to control her nervousness. "I'm planning to assume it again."

"And you decided it would be a good joke to land a job here?" the assistant manager snapped.

"Of course not." Gripping her purse, Sherry lurched to her feet. "I'm broke. That's the truth. I've got bills to pay and I'm willing to work hard. You won't regret hiring me."

A camera flashed. One man held his phone high, as if letting a friend listen to her words. Good gracious, was there no end to people's nerve?

"You don't have the job yet," muttered a man in line ahead of her.

"I meant…*if*."

With an outraged wave, Mrs. Fordyce indicated the knot of rubberneckers at the doorway. "We can't have our customers tied up this way." Her gaze flicked over Sherry's designer purse. "I don't believe we carry your favorite brands, Mrs. LaSalle. Obviously, working here wouldn't suit your interests *or* ours."

The unfairness of the situation hit Sherry right in the gut. *Please don't let me cry in front of all these people.* She didn't want to lose her temper, either.

She reminded herself that Mrs. Fordyce had probably spent years working her way to the assistant manager's position, and resented anyone she believed had life easy. That didn't excuse her cruel behavior, but it was no use arguing a lost cause.

Ignoring the smugness on several faces, Sherry addressed her fellow job seekers. "I'm sorry some of you refuse to believe I'm sincere. Most of you seem like nice people and I wish you good luck."

"Thanks." The skinny girl beamed.

Sherry pivoted—and halted at seeing her exit blocked by a wall of spectators. As if on signal, requests filled the air. "Would you talk to my mother on my phone? She doesn't believe it's really you."

"Will you pose with me?"

"Hey, Sherry, how about a date?"

Although she longed to flee with an urgency bordering on desperation, she wasn't sure how she'd ever get out of there.

"THREE THOUSAND DOLLARS?" Rafe repeated in dismay. "That's your placement fee?" Despite an open window, the car suddenly seemed airless.

"It's really quite reasonable. You have to consider the advertising and screening we do." Judging by the smoothness of her response, the woman at the nanny agency often received this sort of reaction. "We perform background checks, including references and criminal records."

Criminal records. Jeez. Rafe hadn't considered the implications of entrusting his niece and nephew to a stranger. With licensed day cares, the government handled that sort of thing.

Or so he hoped.

"I'll get back to you." He pressed End, and, stretching his legs, surveyed the front of the store. No sign of Sherry. He dialed the next number.

The second agency charged only two thousand dollars, but had already placed everyone on its registry. "We're advertising for new nanny candidates now. Please try us again in a month."

A month? Thirteen-year-old Suzy Ching, his fill-in sitter, might be able to handle the twins for a few days, but certainly not a month. Plus she'd most likely already filled her summer schedule. Kids these days had long lists of activities, he'd heard.

With agency number three, Rafe finally struck pay dirt. Not only did they charge a more affordable fifteen hundred dollars, but after he provided his credit information, they agreed to schedule interviews for their two available nannies. Ginger would stop by Thursday at 6:00 p.m. to meet him and the children, with Mildred reporting later that evening.

Surely one of them would fill the bill. They had been prescreened and both, the woman assured him, had completed child-development courses.

Checking the time, Rafe discovered he'd dallied long enough. Work must be piling up at the garage, and he couldn't expect Mario and Jeb to cover his absence much longer.

He'd better check on Sherry's progress—discreetly, in case she was in the middle of an interview.

When he arrived inside the store, though, Rafe had trouble getting a clerk's attention to ask about the status of the interviews. The first aproned woman he approached kept peering toward the rear of the store, where a bunch of customers were swarming as if there was a once-in-a-lifetime sale happening.

"What's going on?" he asked the salesclerk.

"A celebrity's pretending to apply for a job," she told him. "I'm betting it's a stunt."

The possibility that two notorious personalities had appeared in a Brea discount store on the same day defied the odds. *"I seem to have a talent for causing trouble."* Sherry hadn't been kidding.

As Rafe drew closer, he could barely squeeze between the carts. Around him, women commented excitedly, as if seeing Sherry in person provided a rare form of entertainment. Although there'd been newspaper write-ups almost daily after Winston absconded, it hadn't occurred to Rafe she might have become *that* recognizable.

Finally, over a sea of bobbing heads, he spotted her small figure. Facing his direction, she was trying to angle through the crowd, but people clustered too close, thrusting pens and paper at her and snapping pictures. A couple of women practically manhandled her to get themselves into a shot.

"Clear the way, please," Rafe boomed. "Step aside, ma'am. Excuse me, coming through." To his relief, the shoppers parted.

Sherry gazed at him as if he'd descended in a heavenly chariot. "Thank goodness you're here."

He shook his head at the pandemonium around them. "How on earth did this happen?"

"I'm not sure. Can we go?" Her voice trembled.

"Of course." Clearing a path with a few forceful commands, he escorted her past the onlookers. Amid the buzz that arose, he caught the word *bodyguard.* Someone else muttered, "New boyfriend."

Yeah, right.

Beside him, Sherry walked stiffly. "That must have been terrifying," he said when they'd finally passed the checkout stands and were heading for freedom.

"I'm shaking." She sounded disgusted. "I can't believe I'm reacting this way. I don't know how real celebrities deal with this sort of thing every day."

He refrained from pointing out that, to these locals, she obviously was a celebrity. "Can you make it to the car?"

"Sure. My knees will stop knocking together any time now."

An entering customer stared at them wide-eyed. "Is that really you?" she asked. "Sherry Lasso?"

"No." Outside, she said morosely, "Sherry Lasso. That sure sums up the level of my fame. I'm famous for being sort of vaguely familiar."

Rafe took her arm. "Watch your step on the curb."

She gripped him tightly, then lifted her hand. "I'm okay, but...I can't believe you rescued me."

"Because you assumed I was an ogre?"

"No. Because everybody else treats me like a freak show." Clearly anguished, she gazed up at him. "I can't even land a minimum-wage job. Can you believe that?"

He decided to be frank. "You didn't really think you were suited to waiting on the general public, did you?"

Sherry blinked. "Why not? I'd serve hamburgers or collect shopping carts if that's what it takes to earn a living."

They reached Rafe's car. "It wouldn't take more than a few days of long hours and aching muscles before you'd collapse. And you'd be miserable. Maybe you don't exactly look down on people like me, but..."

"I'd gladly put on a blue jumpsuit and get grease all over my face if I could earn a decent wage." Her face scrunched. "No, I wouldn't. Who am I kidding? My parents brought me up to be useless."

"On that point, we agree." The words slipped out before he could stop them. He didn't mean to be cruel. Still, neither had he forgotten her arrogant attitude of a few months ago.

She gave a startled jerk. "I was exaggerating. The truth is, I've raised a lot of money for charity."

"Because you enjoyed ordering new gowns, attending fancy balls and posing for photographs." Despite feeling some sympathy for her, Rafe doubted this woman had changed much at heart. A whiff of her missing millions and she'd go haring off after her old life.

"No, I didn't! And as for being photographed, I've had enough of that to last me till..." Sherry paused before finishing with rueful honesty, "Till I'm older."

"How much older?"

"At least a week," she conceded.

They both chuckled. The tension popped like an overheated balloon.

"Well, back to work for me," Rafe said. "I've got a car to fix for some rich lady."

"Sorry about that."

"It should be done soon."

He switched on the radio to fill the silence that fell between them. A song accompanied them out of the parking lot, and then a deejay broke in.

"Alert listener Sam Smithers just transmitted this sound bite from Brea. Listen carefully—you won't believe who this is."

Over the speakers came scratchy background noise and then a familiar female voice declared, "I've got bills to pay like everyone else. I'm willing to work hard."

Beside him, Sherry tensed.

"That's dripping-rich society girl Sherry LaSalle, recently scammed by the light of her life." The host sketched the details of the discount store's locale, Sherry's attempt to apply for a job and her ignominious departure. "Truly, folks, I don't make these things up. Also, I heard a dark-haired mystery man appeared at her side and whisked her out of the building. Chauffeur, bodyguard or new love interest?"

"I wish he'd shut up," Sherry moaned.

"Want me to change the station?"

She sighed. "I'd better hear the rest of what this clown has to say."

"Sam wins a gift certificate for a night on the town. Folks, call me—that's Deejay V.J.—with job suggestions for our dim-witted diva," the fellow chortled. "Whoever makes the best suggestion will receive a prize. How about a gift certificate to a local thrift store?

If you're lucky, you might run into Sherry baby working behind the counter."

Rafe nearly laughed at the man's cheekiness. If Sherry hadn't been sitting beside him, he'd have enjoyed this nonsense.

The music returned. They didn't speak again until they reached her house.

"I'll send someone to tow the car later. Do you have any more appointments today?" he asked.

"If I did, I'd cancel them," she said glumly.

Rafe tried but failed to muster a reassuring comment. Instead, he said goodbye and drove off.

Something told him this lady wasn't nearly as dim-witted as the deejay assumed, nor likely to stay crushed for long. In fact, he was kind of rooting for her.

All the same, he planned to keep the radio at the garage tuned to this station.

WRAPPED IN A BEIGE FLEECE blanket, Sherry huddled on her sofa and sipped herbal tea. What a humiliating experience. The worst part was the sneaking sense that she deserved it.

As Rafe had pointed out, she'd indulged in a childish fantasy about working in a discount store. How unrealistic to expect to go unrecognized after that much-publicized mess with Winston. Rafe was also right about her being unprepared for the physical and mental demands of such a job.

Still, he'd gone too far when he claimed she only raised funds as a form of entertainment. Take this blanket, for instance. The Indian village co-op enabled widows to support their families. She and her friend

Becky had had a grand time planning the game nights that had provided the co-op's initial funding.

Oh, Lord, he *was* right. Sure, she'd meant well, but she'd also been indulging herself.

She still needed money, badly. What was she going to do?

Sherry had never had career goals. At nineteen, she'd been attending general education classes in community college when her adoring parents died. If not for their attorney, Elliott LaSalle, she didn't know what she'd have done.

Maybe I could have learned to take care of business instead of glomming onto a guy. Not until later had Sherry discovered that he'd lied about being estranged from his wife. It had taken her even longer to realize that Lynn LaSalle wasn't simply an embittered woman who had trouble accepting the failure of her marriage. She was a loving, middle-aged wife dumped for a younger model.

Seven years later, Elliott had announced out of the blue that he was divorcing Sherry to marry a twenty-two-year-old journalism student who'd interviewed him for a business magazine. Sherry's world had crashed.

She'd never imagined that her husband would do to her what he'd done to his first wife. How blind could a woman be?

That didn't make her a bad person, just a foolish one. She had to get a grip, face the future and prove her detractors wrong.

What *were* they saying about her now? Steeling her nerve, Sherry switched on her mother's old radio.

She didn't have to wait long for another of the deejay's grating sallies. "Folks, my apologies if you haven't been able to get through with your suggestion of jobs for poor little rich girl Sherry LaSalle. Our lines are jammed, but we'll be choosing a winner every hour. Thanks to our generous advertisers, our next gift certificate will be for a beauty makeover at…"

This crummy contest was growing? Sherry grimaced, yet couldn't bring herself to turn off the darn radio.

The deejay tabbed a caller, who contributed, "I'd like to see Sherry become a lion tamer. I mean, that's as realistic as her working as a salesclerk."

"Lion tamer," the announcer repeated. "I don't see any lions on the Web site for the Santa Ana Zoo. But there's an American feral pig and something called a Toggenburg goat. How about letting Ms. LaSalle milk a goat? Or corral a white-faced whistling duck? That ought to ruffle her fine feathers."

This guy might be mildly amusing. *If* he was targeting someone else.

"While we're on an animal theme, here's a proposal for her to dress up in a monkey suit and cheer at Anaheim Angels games. Good one! Keep 'em coming, folks."

As the music resumed, Sherry wondered what the baseball mascot job paid. At least a mask would keep her face hidden.

Well, these people might be joking, but Rafe's lack of faith in her rankled, especially since she'd started to like the guy. Sherry wasn't useless, truly.

Throwing off the blanket, she dug out a pad and pen and set to listing jobs she might be able to do. Positions that didn't require much training and wouldn't put her in front of the public.

She had lots of exciting, creative ideas. Maybe she'd surprise everyone.

Chapter Five

Rafe had hoped to finish Sherry's car that week. Instead, a couple of rush jobs from a used-car dealership that had a contract with the garage kept him and his staff busy. Plus they had their individual customers, as well.

Finally he sent Jeb to patch the tires, because there was no reason for Rafe to have any more contact than necessary with his neighbor.

Despite the tug of compassion he felt, he remained keenly aware of the gap between them. Also, since Sherry would be moving on soon enough, any friendship they formed would be temporary at best. And highly embarrassing at worst. He hadn't forgotten the radio announcer calling him a mystery man. Thank goodness nobody had identified him.

Around four o'clock on Thursday, a yellow car pulled onto the property and halted behind a repair bay. The driver, a copper-haired young woman in a frilly print blouse and beige jeans, sauntered toward him.

"Problem?" Rafe wiped his hands on a rag.

Sunshine highlighted a stellar array of freckles. "I'm looking for Rafe Montoya."

"That would be me."

"I'm Ginger." She regarded him expectantly.

The name went right past him. Then he remembered. "The nanny. We have an appointment at the house. At 6:00 p.m." She could have passed for a high school student, but he recalled her age as nineteen.

"I like to meet my employer away from the children." She jumped as an engine roared behind her.

He'd have preferred it if she hadn't interrupted his work. Still, there was no point in being rude to the woman. "It's kind of noisy here. Let's go inside."

"Oh, this won't take long. Is there anything about the children I should know ahead of time?" Ginger asked. "The agency only gave me their names and ages."

Rafe laid out the facts. "I've adopted my niece and nephew, who were orphaned last year. Their day care's closing and the owner believes they'd benefit from individual attention."

Ginger frowned. "Are they in therapy?"

"They went through that already."

"I gather there are behavioral issues. I mean, I assume that, based on what you say their care provider recommended."

"She suggested individual attention, not psychoanalysis." He wondered if this young woman expected perfect children. "Sofia needs someone to spend time with her, and Juan can be impulsive, if you consider those 'issues.'"

"What do you mean by impulsive?" she pressed.

Might as well tell the whole story. "Juan ran off on Tuesday." At her shocked expression, Rafe added, "He didn't go far. We found him at a neighbor's house, baking cookies."

"Truthfully, Mr. Montoya, I don't think I'm the right

nanny for your family," Ginger said. "Kids with problems ought to get special treatment."

Rafe reined in the temptation to ask what she was implying. "My niece and nephew aren't holy terrors. They're sweet children who've done well considering they lost their parents," he said tightly. "However, you don't seem to be mature enough for the job. Thanks for stopping by."

She regarded him uneasily. "You aren't going to complain to the agency, are you?"

This woman didn't strike him as prime caretaker material. "I'm not sure. It appears you weren't interested in the job in the first place, in which case you've wasted my time."

Without waiting for her response, he returned to his repairs. She beat a fast and probably thankful retreat. He hadn't missed the way her nose wrinkled at the smell of motor oil. This nanny probably hoped to work for one of Orange County's elite families rather than a mechanic.

One nanny down and one to go.

That evening, Rafe picked up Chinese food, both to soothe his annoyance and to put the kids on their best behavior. They loved broccoli with beef and orange chicken.

At 7:59, Mary Poppins arrived on his doorstep. Her real name was Mildred Barlow, but the woman with a touch of gray at the temples charmed him and the children from her first words, which were, "What a wonderful home. And such dear little faces!"

Her references were impressive. Better yet, within minutes she had Sofia cuddled in her lap and Juan perched a mere few inches away as she read from a favorite book.

Her salary ran slightly higher than average because of her level of experience, but she was clearly worth it.

Relieved, Rafe offered her the job on the spot. "You can start Monday, right?"

A shadow crossed her motherly face. "The agency should have explained that I'm not available until September."

"September?" Dismay filled him. She might as well have said Christmas. Or the turn of the next century.

Mildred dabbed her eyes with a lace-trimmed handkerchief. "The family I work for is moving to England this fall. They begged me to come with them, but I can't leave my grown daughter and grandson."

Rafe would have dropped to his knees if he'd thought it might help. "Are you sure you can't start sooner? You're perfect."

"They're darlings." She gazed regretfully at the upturned faces. "I'm sorry about the misunderstanding, Mr. Montoya. I can't possibly start for three months."

Then, to his distress, she left.

Sofia burst into tears. Arms folded, Juan announced, "I want the gingerbread lady!"

"The princess?" his sister asked with interest.

"Yeah."

"Me, too."

For a nanosecond, Rafe considered the possibility of hiring Sherry LaSalle, assuming she'd want the job. She lived nearby and already had the children's vote. There were two good reasons.

On the other hand, she'd never withstand the day-in, day-out responsibility. If she did, she'd probably teach his children the same superficial values her parents had instilled in her.

He had to find a new day care situation, fast.

Shelving his worries, Rafe focused on preparing the kids for bed. After the disappointment over Mrs. Barlow, Sofia held on to him longer than usual and Juan insisted on a second storybook.

By the time they fell asleep, Rafe lacked the energy to launch another search on the Internet or via the Yellow Pages. Instead, he collapsed on the couch.

As always, he enjoyed staring around the large living room with its twelve-foot ceiling and pale orange walls. No matter what Ginger thought, this *was* a mansion compared to the cramped house in Los Angeles where he'd been raised. Still, that house, too, had been filled with love.

Thinking about home reminded Rafe that he hadn't talked to his parents since he and the twins made the hour's drive to visit them on Mother's Day. On that occasion, he'd offered to treat everyone to dinner at a restaurant, but his mom had insisted on cooking. Her enchiladas beat anything he'd ever tasted elsewhere, and the flan she'd fixed for dessert was unforgettable.

Rafe put in the call. His mom, Nina, greeted him contentedly. His father and grandmother were sleeping, and she was in the mood to talk. "How're the kids?" was her first question.

"Fine. Except I need a new sitter." He told her about Maryam's change of plans, the nanny interviews and Juan's silly idea of consulting a witch.

"He ran away?" she asked worriedly.

"Just down the street." He described Juan's visit to Sherry's, which led to recounting the oddball experience at the discount store.

"The poor woman must be humiliated," his mom

said. "I've never understood why people fuss over celebrities. They've got problems like everybody else."

"She'll cope."

"She's already coping. She found a handsome man to drive her around," Nina teased.

"Just that once."

"And a cute little man who likes her gingerbread cookies." Her chuckle tickled Rafe's ear. "She's looking for a job and you're looking for a nanny. You called to get my opinion?"

"I called because I miss you!"

"That's sweet, *mijo.*" The affectionate term was a contraction of the Spanish phrase *mi hijo,* my son. "But usually when you call, it's on a Sunday. When I hear from you during the week, you've got more than chit-chat in mind."

There was no sense arguing. His mom was right: he *did* want her opinion. "You've heard me complaining about this woman for months. She's the last person I'd entrust with the kids."

"That's true," his mother said calmly. "A snob like that will drive you crazy."

Her reaction disappointed him. "She may be sheltered, but she has a kind heart. And Juan took to her at once. You should have heard him singing along with her."

"Like he used to do with his mama," she murmured.

"That's right." He'd almost forgotten that Cara used to play his father's old guitar at family events.

"Still, you can't let him get attached to a neighbor who's playful and has fancy friends."

"I'm not sure she has any friends left," Rafe corrected. "And what's wrong with being playful?"

"No matter what I say about her, you argue with me," his mom responded. "You should hire her."

"You tricked me!"

"I played devil's advocate," she countered. "It's a good technique for discovering the truth."

Rafe bristled. "I don't want to hire her. The kids deserve better than to get dumped as soon as the novelty wears thin."

"You said you needed someone only until September."

"I only need someone *full-time* until September." What did families do about their nannies once the kids started school? he wondered.

"Sleep on it," Nina advised. "You'll have your answer."

"Or bad dreams."

"I doubt that," she told him. "Speaking of the twins, we'll celebrate their birthday next month. Should I fix flan or chocolate cake or both?"

"Is that a serious question?"

She laughed. "Okay, both."

"Why can't I meet a woman like you?" Rafe complained.

"You already have a woman like me—I'm right here. Now you deserve someone younger and prettier, so broaden your horizons," his mother retorted. "A man like you isn't meant to live alone, *mijo.*"

"I don't live alone. And I've got a busy social life." That might be a slight exaggeration, but he played softball with J. J. Hughes and went to baseball games with Josh Lorenz from up the block. Before taking in the kids, he'd dated occasionally, although the relationships always seemed to fizzle after a few months.

His mother yawned audibly. "Sorry. I guess I'm more tired than I thought. Kiss my grandchildren for me."

"With pleasure."

He decided to follow her suggestion about sleeping on the matter of hiring Sherry, not that it would make any difference. A bad idea was a bad idea, even in the morning light.

ON FRIDAY, Sherry took a hard look at the list she'd drawn up, and threw it in the trash.

She couldn't open a gift shop without investment capital. Ditto for launching a catering service. Besides, customers would expect more than a few specialties like gingerbread men. As for giving music lessons, she hadn't a clue where to begin. Did kids want to read music anymore, or did they simply learn chords?

If only the feds would nab Winston, she'd be thrilled to recover any part of her fortune. A simple million would let her drop this dreary business of finding a job, and enroll in college, which she'd concluded was a wise idea.

Well, at least she had her own beloved car back. Earlier this morning, a man from Rafe's garage had called to say it was ready. She'd gladly driven over on her recently repaired tires, and claimed her sedan, with its whisper-smooth ride and state-of-the-art sound system. Sherry felt almost like her old self again.

She'd been disappointed at failing to spot Rafe, whom she'd wanted to thank. He'd been out test-driving a car, the mechanic said.

Instead, she jotted a thank-you note and addressed it in care of the garage. Leaving it on his porch seemed inadequate.

Sherry went outside to put it in her mailbox. Too late for today. The delivery had already arrived.

Sorting through the circulars and bills she found in it, she wandered back inside. Another credit card statement already? She could manage the minimum payment, the same way she had last month.

A sentence on the bill confused Sherry. What did that mean—over the limit? She hadn't known there *was* a limit. Oh, for heaven's sake! Not only had she exceeded it, but they'd charged a forty-dollar penalty.

The paper slipped from her fingers. She stood there trying to absorb the implications.

She had to stop charging things. Moreover, even if she could get a minimum-wage job, she'd be forced to work for *hours* just to pay the penalty.

How childish it was for her to fantasize about the authorities nabbing her ex-fiancé, or that she'd be blithely off to earn a college degree anytime soon. If she understood this penalty business, she was running up debt by simply standing here breathing.

As a last resort, she supposed she could sell the diamond earrings, which ought to be worth a few thousand dollars, but her stomach knotted at the prospect of losing that link to her parents.

Then Sherry got an idea.

A sign down the street advertised a home day care center. Surely lots of people brought their children during the summer, so perhaps the woman who ran it could use an assistant. Her name, Sherry recalled, was Maryam Hughes, and her husband served on the association board of directors.

Reluctant to waste a moment, she ran to the bathroom

and dragged a brush through her hair. She was overdue for a trim, which she didn't dare add to the charges on her card. Instead, she twisted the shaggy strands into a bun.

Ready to go. And this time, she couldn't afford to fail.

Chapter Six

Approaching Maryam's two-story house, Sherry recalled that the woman had signed a petition to prevent the cottage from being torn down. She would most likely slam the door when she saw who was standing on the other side.

Take a deep breath. Don't give up before you've started.

Once, Sherry had asked Winston how, in his early years as a consultant and developer, he'd survived the inevitable rejections. He'd smiled indulgently. "Rejections don't matter," he'd told her. "They're nothing but stepping stones on the road to success."

In his case, stepping stones on the road to con jobs. Nevertheless, he'd had a point.

Sherry marched to the front door and rang the bell. Then she reminded herself to breathe again before she passed out.

A tall woman appeared in the doorway. "Yes?"

Struggling to keep her voice steady, Sherry said, "I don't know if you remember me.... I guess you do, huh?"

"Kind of hard not to," Maryam said coolly.

Sherry decided to blurt her purpose before she chickened out. "I'm looking for a job. Temporary is fine."

Had she omitted something? "I like kids and I thought you might need help for the summer."

Maryam moved aside. "Come in."

Sherry entered the tiled entryway and gazed into the large, colorful living room. It was the first time she'd entered a house in Harmony Circle except for her own and Minnie's, she realized.

Only a few months ago, accustomed to living in mansions, she'd dismissed these tract homes as small and ordinary. She'd never have chosen to live here if she'd had anywhere else to go. Now, compared to her bungalow, Maryam's place appeared spacious and intriguing, with its high ceilings and mix of antique and modern furnishings. "What a beautiful place."

"Hardly up to your standards," the woman replied stiffly.

"I love decor with personality," Sherry assured her. "I'd much rather see things people picked out of love than because of a design scheme."

Maryam thawed a few degrees. "That definitely describes my style. But as for hiring you…"

A little girl trotted in. "Mommy, Sofia took my doll."

"Well, Coretta, I would just ask her to give it back."

Her daughter thought about this for a moment. "Okay," she said, and off she went.

How simple, direct and effective. "That was great, the way you empowered her."

"Is that what I did?" Maryam asked.

"You gave her the tools to solve the problem herself." Eagerness welled inside Sherry. What fun to work with kids and watch them develop. She'd never considered that she might actually *enjoy* a job.

Maryam's next words doused her hopes. "I'm closing the center. My mother suffered a stroke and I'll be helping her for as long as she needs it. My husband's picking her up at the hospital this afternoon. I'd have gone, too, but I couldn't on such short notice—it's my last day with the kids."

Sherry tried not to show her disappointment. "How wonderful of you to take care of her."

"She's my mom. Anybody would do the same."

"Yes, absolutely. If my parents were alive, I'd drop everything to be with them." The children's noises grew louder, reminding Sherry of her purpose. "Do you suppose any of them need private sitters?"

"One of my clients is putting her kids in a church-sponsored program," Maryam told her. "I'm not sure if Rafe Montoya has found anybody. Of course, you guys have a history, don't you?"

"Kind of like the Hundred Years' War," Sherry conceded. "I did have fun playing with Juan, though. If there's anything I can do to help you or your mom, please call. I don't mean as a job, just as a neighbor."

"That's sweet," Maryam said. "If anyone asks me about a sitter, I'll suggest you. Of course, if you plan to watch more than one or two kids in your home on a regular basis, the county requires a license."

Sherry hadn't thought that far ahead. "Is it complicated?"

"You have to install safety equipment, develop an emergency plan and learn CPR," Maryam advised. "There are classes you can go to."

"I don't think I'm ready for that." While taking all

that training sounded great, Sherry needed a job *now,* plus safety equipment sounded expensive.

"Good luck with whatever you do," Maryam said, sounding genuine.

"I'll stay in touch, if it's okay."

"I'd like that."

Grateful for the positive note, Sherry took her leave. She'd have enjoyed saying hi to Juan, but preferred not to disturb the children.

Outside, she inhaled the scent of jasmine from next door. What a pretty street this was. When she'd first seen it the day Oliver brought her to view the cottage, she'd longed to settle here and raise the children she and Winston had planned to have.

Or, rather, that *she'd* planned. Everything, other than this neighborhood, had been a mirage. This was real.

Speaking of reality, she wondered how much baby-sitters earned. Not much, she supposed. Still, Sherry would work hard, including evenings and weekends. If she could land a few regular clients, that might tide her over for a while.

She knocked at Minnie's cottage. A lively face topped by white hair appeared at the window, then her neighbor hurried to admit her.

"What's the latest?" In her eighties, Minnie made few concessions to age beyond the color of her hair and the stoop of her shoulders. "Hope you haven't run into any more ogres disguised as interviewers."

Relieved to find a sympathetic ear, Sherry had kept her neighbor informed of her job search. "I've decided I'd really like to babysit. I adore kids and I think I'd be good at it."

"Excellent timing. Maryam next door is closing shop," she reported. Too bad Sherry hadn't consulted Minnie first.

"I just talked to her." In the cozy living room, which was slightly larger than her own, Sherry studied a photo of Minnie's seven-month-old great-granddaughter. "This is new, isn't it? What a precious outfit."

They discussed the baby's progress—she'd begun babbling and crawling—before returning to Sherry's issue. "Could you suggest anyone who might need a sitter?"

"Oliver and Brooke, after their baby's born."

"That won't be for months." *And Brooke wouldn't hire me if I were the last babysitter in Southern California.*

"True. Let me see." Reviewing a mental list, Minnie accounted for the other residents of their street. In addition to newlyweds Diane and Josh Lorenz, who both had twelve-year-old daughters from previous marriages, she mentioned a group of women who'd designated themselves the Foxes, which stood for Females Only—Exuberantly Single.

"Diane and Brooke are honorary members, even though they've gotten married," Minnie said. "We meet once a month for potlucks and gossip."

Sherry didn't inquire who the Foxes gossiped about, since she had a pretty good idea of the answer. "No divorced mothers?" They'd probably be her best bet.

"Jane McKay would love to have a baby whether she finds a husband first or not, but I don't suppose that counts. She's an obstetrician. Must be hard, delivering babies every day when you're longing for a child of your own."

"That does sound hard." Sherry wondered which of the people at that home-owners meeting had been Jane.

The woman who came to mind had had a wistful manner and an open expression. *I'll bet I'd like her.* "What about elsewhere in the development?"

"Nobody I can think of, but you might print some fliers."

"Just imagine if that radio station got hold of them. Thanks for trying, though."

"Stop by anytime." Minnie patted her hands reassuringly. "Something will work out. You'll see."

"I'm certain it will."

Maybe, Sherry reflected as she departed, she should contact additional employment agencies. Or pay attention to the crazy jobs proposed on the radio.

Wearing a monkey suit was beginning to sound like a viable career option.

USUALLY THE KIDS SCARFED down macaroni and cheese and begged for more. Tonight, neither Juan nor Sofia consumed more than a few bites.

"No dessert till you finish your meal." Rafe indicated the peas and carrots they hadn't touched. "At least eat the vegetables."

The two of them just sat there. If they stared at their plates any harder, the peas and carrots might explode.

"I realize it was your last day at Mrs. Hughes', but you'll still be able to play with Luther and Coretta," he said.

"Who's gonna watch us?" Juan demanded.

"I told you, the Panda Preschool." The popular local facility had small classes, which were full. However, the director had recommended that Rafe bring the children on Monday, the start of the summer term, since registrants often failed to appear.

A tear rolled down Sofia's cheek. "I want to stay home."

"Me, too," said her brother.

"I have to work, and I can't leave you alone." Frustrated, Rafe contemplated ordering them to eat, but he'd never liked the idea of forcing food down kids' throats. "The heck with it. I'll reheat these later." He grabbed the plates and thrust them into the refrigerator. "As long as your stomachs are empty, who wants to go swimming?"

Normally they clamored to play in the community pool, but today, they hung on to their pouts for several seconds before Juan said, "We can swim at night?"

"There's daylight for a couple more hours." The pool remained open until 8:00 p.m. Before becoming a parent, Rafe had often gone for a dip after work.

"Tomorrow," Sofia said.

He wanted to distract them *tonight.* "This offer isn't good tomorrow."

"Why not?"

There *was* a reason, Rafe recalled. "We're going to play miniature golf with Oliver and Brooke."

Juan poked his sister. "Let's go."

She leveled a stare at her twin. It reminded Rafe of his mother's expression when he used to exasperate her.

Juan sweetened the deal. "You can play with my squirt gun."

"Only if you can do it without bothering anyone else," Rafe cautioned.

Sofia considered the offer. "Okay."

The kids raced to their rooms. Rafe made a mental note to buy his niece her own squirt gun for her birthday. He'd been keeping track of their favorite toys, with help from Maryam.

He sure was going to miss her input. He doubted a preschool, even an excellent one, would offer the same personalized and friendly service.

Within minutes, the children had wriggled into their suits and grabbed towels and toys. Rafe, wearing a T-shirt pulled over his trunks, led them to the car. Although the pool was only a few blocks away, the air cooled rapidly at night and he didn't want the kids walking home in wet outfits.

The price of driving was listening to Juan whoop siren noises the whole way. That boy loved riding in a converted cop car.

Only a few swimmers broke the water, Rafe noted as he pulled into the parking lot. At the wrought-iron gate, he let Sofia swipe the magnetic card key.

"Nobody goes in the water till I'm ready," he called as the kids bolted ahead of him. "And no running. You might slip."

They slowed to watch a couple of teenage boys swimming laps. Then Juan called, "Hey, it's the gingerbread lady," and hurried toward a woman standing beside a lounge chair, partly obscured by a towel.

Sherry LaSalle must have just emerged from the water, judging by the droplets trickling down her shapely legs. She was toweling her hair, seemingly unaware of the picture she presented in a pale pink bikini that nearly disappeared against her skin.

Rafe's body hardened as he took in her round breasts and slender waist. He muttered a few angry words at this unwanted reaction, particularly in revealing swim trunks.

Keeping his towel in front of him, he approached

Sherry. Although he was reluctant to become too well acquainted with her, he could hardly ignore her.

"Hi." She straightened after greeting the children. "I didn't expect... What're you..." She swallowed. Why was she so nervous? Rafe wondered.

Juan tugged her hand. "Come play with us."

"Yes, please," Sofia joined in.

Sherry regarded Rafe. "Is it all right?"

He could hardly object to her splashing about with the children. "If that's what my niece and nephew want, be my guest."

Juan cheered. Sofia beamed.

Rafe deposited their gear next to some chairs while the threesome sauntered toward the shallow end. Even without designer clothes, Sherry exuded elegance. He tried to identify what it was about her—her graceful walk, the straight, confident shoulders—but couldn't pinpoint it.

She simply radiated sophistication. It was no wonder, really, when she'd been born to luxury. Yet she seemed genuinely interested in the children as she and Sofia descended the steps into the pool. Ahead of them, Juan demonstrated the dog paddle and called to Sherry for praise, which she willingly bestowed.

Rafe wished he could figure her out; she was full of contradictions.

And she sure looked great in a bikini.

AFTER A LIGHT DINNER, Sherry had suffered an attack of Friday-night cabin fever. She'd chosen to visit the pool partly because it was free entertainment, and also because she needed the exercise now that she'd given up her gym membership.

She hoped Rafe hadn't noticed her breathlessness when she'd caught sight of him. He had a great build, and the fact that he remained single despite those striking dark looks raised suspicions about the sanity of her unmarried neighbors.

Well, she'd better cut the starry-eyed nonsense. Experience had taught Sherry to mistrust her instincts where men were concerned.

"I get the squirt gun," Sofia told her brother, who was filling it beneath the surface.

"Okay. But not the *whole* time." He didn't release it. Not yet.

The clang of the gate marked the exit of the older boys, leaving Sherry, Rafe and the children alone. "I hope you aren't planning to squirt *me,*" Sherry declared, fully aware that her statement tempted fate.

Sure enough, Juan lifted the plastic pistol and fired a stream of water into her stomach. He giggled madly.

"My turn!" Sofa cried. Reluctantly, her brother surrendered the gun.

"Now that you're unarmed," Sherry said, "I owe you one." With the heel of her hand, she sent a spray of water over the little boy. "Gotcha!"

He emerged spluttering but fascinated. "How'd you learn to do that?"

"I used to be a kid, too. My dad taught me."

Sofia, who'd quietly refilled the gun, pointed it at Sherry. "If I shoot you, are you gonna spray me?"

"Fair's fair," Sherry said.

Instead, Sofia sprayed her brother. He tried to retaliate by hitting the water, but raised only a few drops.

"Nice try," Sherry told him.

"Show me how!"

"First let's put down the water gun, okay?" She removed it to the concrete lip of the pool. "Now, do this." She demonstrated how to hit the surface fast and hard. The children gleefully followed suit.

Amid the rowdiness, Sherry lost track of Rafe until a tsunami rolled over the shallow end. As she and the children scrubbed their faces of water, she spotted Rafe, who must have cannonballed. "Sorry," he called with mock innocence. "Did I splash you guys?"

"No, you drowned us," Sherry said, laughing.

"Get Uncle Rafe!" Juan aimed a series of tiny waves at the man, who, undaunted, rose from the spray like a Greek statue. Intimidated, the boy backed off.

"I'm not going to soak you," Rafe assured him.

"Horsey ride?" his nephew asked.

"Later, okay?"

"Sure." Juan ducked his head, disappointed.

Catching Juan off guard, Rafe picked him up and swung him in a circle. "Had enough?"

"Me! Me!" Sofia cried, until he gave her a whirl, too.

What a great guy, Sherry thought. He hadn't asked to be a dad, but he was devoted to the kids. What a contrast to her self-absorbed first husband and heartless fiancé.

A faceful of water washed away her reverie. When her vision cleared, she saw Rafe grinning, while the twins stood on the steps watching in delight. "You expect me to leave you standing there like a bathing beauty?" Rafe teased.

Determined not to allow his size to faze her, Sherry swiveled, flopped onto her stomach and kicked the water, hard. From behind came a satisfying "Hey! No fair."

"Totally fair." She soon stopped, though. To prevent a resumption of their playful battle, she scooped up an inflated ball from the side of the pool, where the kids had left it. "Anyone for catch?"

Everyone agreed, and the ball flew. What with leaping, swimming and fetching it from poolside, the children tired quickly.

Once they began complaining, Sofia accompanied Sherry out of the water, while Rafe gave Juan a brief horsey ride and then set him on the edge of the pool. "There you go, sport."

The boy jumped right in again, landing against his uncle's chest and knocking him off balance. "More!"

Rafe found his footing. "Don't mess around in the water. If I'd slipped the wrong way, you'd have hit your head on the concrete." He set the boy on the steps. "Pool time's over."

"You're mean." Pouting, Juan hurried to Sherry's side. "Isn't he?"

Much as she valued the boy's good opinion, she refused to take sides against Rafe. "Your father's right."

"He's not my father!"

She'd misspoken. Still, Rafe *had* adopted the children. "I know, sweetie, but your uncle loves you. That's why he cares about your safety. So please listen to him."

Juan sulked for a bit. Finally he relented. "Okay."

Casting her an appreciative glance, Rafe wrapped himself in a towel. Quietly, to Sherry, he said, "You're good with them."

"Thanks." She hesitated, but only for a second, because if she waited any longer she might lose heart. "Have you found a new day care for them?"

"How did you know I needed one?"

"I asked Maryam about working for her. She explained that she's closing down." Sherry tied the sash of her terry-cloth cover-up. "So...have you?"

"Not exactly." He kept his tone low. "We're on the waiting list at a preschool."

Sherry's pulse sped. *Do it now.* "Hire me," she said, and braced for his response.

Chapter Seven

Rafe believed that when a person thought an issue through and arrived at a rational conclusion, he should stick by it. Impulsiveness led to mistakes, sometimes serious ones.

When he purchased his garage from the man who'd been his boss for six years, old Charley had insisted on a price higher than Rafe had determined was fair. Rafe had stuck to his guns, and after a tense few days of deliberation, Charley had yielded.

Well, Rafe had decided long ago that associating with Sherry LaSalle—and that included entrusting her with his kids—was a bad idea. Still, rejecting her request outright would be rude. And she *had* handled them well tonight. "I'll need to think about it." Not a brilliant response, but sensible.

She gave a tight nod, obviously on tenterhooks.

Rafe didn't mean to keep her waiting longer than necessary, knowing how difficult that could be. "I'll drive you home," he added. "We can put the kids to bed and talk."

She visibly relaxed, then nodded again.

The children fell asleep almost as soon as he tucked

them in. Returning to the living room in clean clothes, Rafe felt an odd sense of rightness when he saw Sherry curled on the couch, cheek resting on a cushion, her terry-cloth cover-up pulled around her.

"Penny for your thoughts." He chose an easy chair across from her, deliberately putting space between them.

She sat up. "You aren't going to hire me," she told him resignedly.

"What makes you say that?"

"The way you look at me."

He wondered what she meant. "I don't dislike you. Not any longer."

"You don't consider me a responsible adult, either." She tugged her robe tighter, accidentally calling attention to the cleavage revealed by her bikini. "I'm not mad. It just would have been a dream job."

They were discussing her working as his nanny, not hosting a beauty infomercial. "A dream job for *you?* You're kidding."

"No. I adore kids, especially yours." Sherry ducked her head with a vulnerability that caught Rafe off guard.

At this moment, she seemed nothing like the Sherry LaSalle who'd lorded over her neighbors and hung on to the arm of her pompous fiancé. The lady in front of him was earnest and kindhearted.

Which was the real her? Or had she changed subconsciously to suit her surroundings?

One thing Rafe believed: she genuinely liked his niece and nephew.

"I can't afford to pay a lot." Now what had made him say that? It almost sounded as if he was considering hiring her.

"I'm aware that nannies don't rank high on the wage scale." She wrapped her arms around her knees, keeping her slender legs angled away from him. "Since you *aren't* my boss, I'm going to offer a suggestion."

"You're handing out parenting advice?" The notion amused him.

"In your case, yes."

This ought to be interesting. "Don't let my blatant skepticism stop you."

"I won't," she said. "Rafe, please start calling the twins your son and daughter instead of your niece and nephew. They might fuss at first, but it's important."

"Why do you think that?"

"In the long run, it could affect their sense of security."

Maryam had also cited the twins' need for stability, Rafe recalled. Still, he had no intention of trying to steal his brother's place in their affections. "I grant you, they're still adjusting to the circumstances, but this hardly seems like your area of expertise."

"It isn't," Sherry conceded, "but I keep remembering what happened to a good friend of mine—well, ex-friend."

Intrigued, he decided to hear her out. "Go ahead."

"When she was little, her dad left and she grew up with a stepdad," Sherry explained. "He always referred to her as his stepdaughter, while he called her younger half sister his daughter. As a result, she believed he was merely tolerating her for her mother's sake."

"Surely his behavior spoke louder than words," Rafe responded.

"Behavior can be open to interpretation. Plus, apparently he had a reserved personality." A pucker formed between Sherry's brows. "When Becky was seventeen, her stepdad died in a car crash. At the funeral, his friends told her how proud he'd been of her accomplishments. He used to carry around school newspaper clippings and report cards and brag about her."

"She had no idea?"

"When he paid her the occasional compliment, she assumed that was to please her mom. Now she wishes she'd been closer to him while he was alive." Sherry pressed her point. "Little things resonate deeply with a child. You're the only father Juan and Sofia have now. Calling them your son and daughter could be reassuring and let them know how much you care."

Doing so seemed awkward. Yet if he'd learned anything in the past year, it was how adaptable kids were, and he *did* want them to accept this situation as permanent. "If you really think they'll benefit, I'll give it a try."

"You're a good dad," Sherry said.

Uncertain how to respond, Rafe changed the subject. "By the way, how come Becky's an *ex*-friend? Did Winston rip her off?"

He almost regretted asking when he saw the shadow in Sherry's eyes. "No. You might say I lost her in the divorce. Elliott insisted everyone choose sides, and her husband's his golfing buddy."

What a preposterous notion, dividing up acquaintances as if they were pieces of furniture. "Isn't she entitled to her own friends?"

"She might be if she felt like an equal," Sherry answered. "Becky's much younger than Abe. She was a struggling singer, and he has a lot of money. She's always catered to him."

Rafe didn't understand why a man would put his

wife in such a subservient position. "Is that what your first marriage was like?"

Sherry hugged a pillow as if it was a stuffed animal. "Not exactly. I had my own money and a certain position in society because of my parents. I scoffed at the people who regarded me as Elliott's trophy wife, but they were right. When he found a younger, prettier specimen, out I went."

It was on the tip of his tongue to say that Elliott couldn't have found a prettier companion, but Rafe stopped. He wasn't romancing this woman. He was hiring her. In spite of his reservations, and probably to the shock of everyone he knew.

He might regret this, but the children doted on her, and Sherry's idea of calling them his son and daughter revealed a lot more maturity than he'd expected. She might be the best caretaker he could hope for.

That was assuming she wouldn't quickly tire of the responsibility or jeopardize the kids in some way. Such as how she'd entertained Juan without considering that people might be searching for him.

"A month," Rafe said.

"Excuse me?"

"I'll hire you on probation for a month," he told her. "If all goes well, you can stay on for another month until school starts, and then afternoons and occasional Saturdays for as long as you're available. If that suits you."

She clenched her hands in her lap. "Yes, it does. Thank you." She seemed afraid to move, as if he might change his mind.

"I realize a temporary position doesn't exactly solve your financial problems," he remarked.

"It'll give me breathing room." She met his gaze squarely. "Rafe, I can't promise to be the best nanny in the history of Brea, but I'll give it everything I've got."

"I'm sure you will." He felt more and more certain of that.

"Thank you," she said, "for trusting me."

"Hey, this suits us both. By the way, I'd better warn you that kids have a way of testing boundaries." She seemed a bit on the sensitive side. "It won't be all playtime. You'll have to keep them in line."

"I can do that," she said confidently.

"Even if they yell, 'I hate you'?"

Sherry flinched. "I might cry. Is guilt manipulation acceptable?"

Rafe laughed. "Whatever works."

"I—" she stifled a yawn "—guess I'd better hit the sack."

They both got to their feet. "See you Monday morning at eight. Not too early, I trust?"

"I'm an early riser, and I'm eager to get started." For an instant, Rafe feared she might launch herself against him for a thank-you hug. He was far too aware of the almost-bare curves beneath her loosely belted robe, and embarrassed by the possibility of her noting his masculine response.

Instead, however, Sherry snatched her towel from the back of a chair. Straining to keep his breathing in check, Rafe walked her to the porch.

He ought to accompany her across the street, but he didn't want to leave the kids alone. Besides, if he saw her to her door, he might take her in his arms and test the electricity between them.

So he said good-night and watched until the lights came on in her house. Darn, that place seemed more like an enchanted cottage every day.

Rafe fetched a beer from the fridge. It was hard to believe Sherry LaSalle had agreed to work as his nanny, he mused as he went to watch the evening news. She seemed to be looking forward to the job, as if she'd put her former life completely aside.

As far as he could tell, it was healthier for her to live in the present instead of dwelling on the past. If that meant she would easily forget him and his children once she recovered her money, well, at least he was prepared. Besides, it also meant she wasn't moping about missing some fashion show or having spa treatments with Orange County's spoiled elite.

He certainly didn't regret his decision to hire her. In the short term, this situation suited everyone.

He tried to imagine how his friends would react when they heard. With raucous laughter or stares of disbelief? And heaven help him if that annoying Deejay V.J. learned of this.

Still, Rafe had never let people's opinions dictate his actions, and he wasn't about to start now.

SHERRY WATCHED HER favorite movie, *The Sound of Music,* and identified more strongly than ever with Maria. Afterward, she slept restlessly, awakening with a vague recollection of childish songfests and a commanding male presence.

Christopher Plummer or Rafe? They'd merged in her dreams.

The important part was to establish a solid relationship with the children, and to have fun with them. She could hardly wait for Monday morning, but she had to get through the whole weekend first.

On Saturday, Sherry awoke early and decided to go for a walk, since few neighbors were likely to be up at this hour. She still felt shy about meeting everyone after her earlier behavior.

She set out in jeans and a T-shirt. A trace of fog veiled the neighborhood, and in the quiet, her shoes made a soft sucking noise against the sidewalk.

The sharp scent of a cigarette hit Sherry's nose before she spotted someone on Maryam's porch. A cigarette dangled from the mouth of a sixtyish woman who was angling her wheelchair onto a newly constructed ramp that led to the walkway.

Maryam's mother must have arrived, but why was she outside alone so soon after her release from the hospital?

As Sherry approached, the woman's wheelchair caught on the rim of the ramp. When the irritated occupant shifted her weight, the chair tipped alarmingly.

"Don't move! You'll fall." Sherry ran forward.

From the opposite direction, a red sports car pulled up to the curb and a striking woman with a wavy golden mane climbed out. She also hurried toward the porch. Sherry recognized the newcomer as Renée Trent, a hairdresser who owned a house at the upper end of the street.

Neither of them wasted time on pleasantries. Renée braced the wheelchair from below, while Sherry stepped onto the ramp and grabbed the opposite side of the chair. "Are you all right?" she asked the woman.

The older lady removed her cigarette. "Yes. Thank

you both. This is terribly embarrassing. I was trying to go for a little stroll by myself."

The stroke clearly hadn't affected her ability to talk, Sherry noted, as she and Renée eased the wheelchair onto the porch. They introduced themselves, and Maryam's mother, whose name was Andrea Brownlee, explained her condition.

"Stroke victims aren't supposed to smoke," Renée chided.

"That's why I'm sneaking around. My daughter would scold me if she caught me."

Sherry warmed to the newcomer, liking Andrea's mischievous streak and determination.

"I worked in a convalescent home while I was in beauty school," the hairdresser continued. "If you don't cut that out, you could have another one."

"Another cigarette?" Andrea feigned hopefulness.

"You know perfectly well what I mean."

The older woman sighed. "I'm trying to quit, believe me. I just got this powerful craving and figured one more time couldn't hurt."

Renée planted her hands on her hips. "You realize we have to tell your daughter."

"I pay bribes," Andrea joked. "How do you feel about free movie tickets?"

Sherry laughed. "I like your sense of humor."

Solemn-faced, Renée reached for the cigarette. "Let me put that out for you."

"Oh, be a sport," Andrea said, then froze when Maryam appeared in the doorway.

"Mom?" She took in the scene. "You're sneaking a smoke?"

"And nearly falling on my butt. These two women saved me from tipping off the ramp," her mother responded. "Have you met Renée and Sherry?"

"Yes. They're good neighbors." Maryam descended to collect the cigarette. "Mom, you heard the doctor. I'm counting on you to set a good example for your grandchildren."

Andrea nodded glumly. "Do they have AA meetings for smokers?"

"Nicotine Anonymous," Renée advised. "I used to smoke, too. You can find a chapter on the Internet."

"I'll do that, if my daughter's willing to drive me to meetings."

"Sure I will." Maryam swiveled the wheelchair toward the house. "Bye, ladies. And thanks."

"Our pleasure. Please get well," Sherry told Andrea.

"I intend to."

Left alone with Renée, Sherry wasn't sure what to say. A close friend of Brooke's, the hairdresser presumably knew about their earlier altercation.

Renée sauntered alongside her to the sidewalk. "I'm glad we both spotted her. That wheelchair was too heavy for either of us."

"She gave me quite a start," Sherry said. "I'm not usually out for a walk at this hour, so it was lucky timing."

"I don't normally start work this early, either. One of my clients called in a panic for a color correction, and this was the only time I could work her in." Renée shook her head. "She was experimenting with an off-brand dye and it turned her hair orange. This isn't the first time she's done something like that."

"What color was it supposed to be?" Sherry asked.

"Burgundy. She should have run a strand test first."

Chatting with Renée made Sherry realize how she missed having girlfriends more than ever. "I like the shade of your hair. It's very flattering."

"It used to be light brown. Bo-oring." Renée stopped beside her car. "Yours is natural, right? You're lucky. Women pay big money for that shade, and it's never quite as pretty as the real thing."

Sherry acknowledged the irony. "I could have afforded any color job I wanted, so it was wasted on me. Now I'm grateful not to have dark roots. My hair's a shaggy enough mess as it is."

"Your old hairdresser must have been expensive," Renée said.

Sherry didn't mind her bluntness. She had no use for polite pretenses, anyway. "I can't afford *any* hairdresser. Fortunately, I just got hired as a nanny—" might as well spill the truth since it would get around soon enough "—working for Rafe Montoya, so I might be able to afford a haircut again soon."

"Seriously?"

"Yes. His niece and nephew are darling, and I'm looking forward to taking care of them."

Renée waved her hand. "I didn't mean to sound surprised. I meant not being able to afford a haircut. You shouldn't have to pay."

That was news to Sherry. "Why not?"

"You're famous!" The woman spoke as if that were an obvious fact. "As a client, you'd be good for business, especially with all the fuss on the radio. How about a trade? I'll trim your hair if you'll let me photograph the results and post your picture in the window."

What a strange notion. "You think women would come to your salon just because I do?" Wryly, she said, "They might pitch tomatoes at the window."

"Don't be ridiculous. You haven't done anything wrong." Renée dismissed the notion briskly. "I'll throw in a free trim for Rafe's niece, too. She's adorable."

Sofia should enjoy the attention. "That's kind of you." Then Sherry paused in concern. "You can't use her picture, though."

"Wouldn't dream of it." Renée handed her a business card. "Give me a call and we'll set up an appointment."

"Terrific." Slightly dazed by the unexpected generosity, Sherry watched the hairdresser stride to her car. What a remarkable woman, affable and businesslike at the same time. And she hadn't even mentioned Brooke. What a relief.

Feeling less apprehensive about her neighbors' responses, Sherry continued up the street. On the corner, Renée's house lay to her right, while on the left, the scents of vanilla and lemon wafted from a two-story home. She'd heard that the teenager who lived there ran a small baking business from her mom's kitchen.

Continuing onward, Sherry turned onto the road that cut across the open end of the U. This high stretch provided a view over the sloping terrain, between stucco houses and flowering yards to the twin cottages below. Gratitude filled Sherry that in spite of everything she'd lost, she'd retained such a lovely home, and that she hadn't been able to destroy it before she learned how beautiful it was.

She didn't spot anyone on the final leg of her stroll. At home, she retrieved her newspaper and settled on the sofa. The paper ran a gardening section on Saturdays, so she didn't expect society photos. Still, as she flipped a page, her eye flew to an item promoting a miniature-golf tournament at noon today on behalf of the Orange County Children's Fund.

Listed among the organizers were Becky Rosen and Helen Salonica. A wave of yearning to be with her friends caught Sherry.

Better to concentrate on new interests. She had a lot to learn before Monday. Going to her desk, Sherry switched on the computer.

Her search revealed a range of child-development programs available at California State University in Fullerton, a mere fifteen-minute drive from Harmony Circle. Although even modest tuition lay beyond her current budget, the discovery gave her a goal to shoot for.

In the meantime, Sherry accessed a site that reviewed the skills expected of children entering kindergarten. She resolved to work on them with Juan and Sofia during the rest of the summer so they'd be ready for school come fall.

After lunch, she drove to the Brea library and checked out volumes on child development. According to the books, children achieved half their ultimate adult intelligence by the age of four, and laid the foundation for their personalities during the first five years. Those bits of trivia weren't nearly as helpful, though, as the information that, for children to learn, they needed to process information through all five of their senses.

Sherry would never have suspected that baking gingerbread men might be an educational experience. What a great reason to do more cooking and baking with the kids. Excited by what she'd discovered, she picked out recipes to try during the next few months.

When the phone rang around three o'clock, she answered warily. A call used to mean an invitation or the opportunity to chat. Lately, she lived with the fear that the press would get hold of her unlisted number.

The deep timbre of Rafe's voice dispelled that concern. "I don't mean to intrude on your weekend," he began.

"Intrude as much as you like." Oops. She didn't wish to seem too eager. "I mean, I wasn't doing anything important."

"Oliver and his wife had to cancel our plans to play miniature golf. It occurred to me that a joint outing might be a good idea," he said. "We can talk about activities to do with the kids, and make sure we're on the same page. I'll pay for your time, of course."

Did it have to be miniature golf? Sherry knew of only one course close by, and she'd rather not run into her old acquaintances. But the tournament had started hours ago, which meant it should have ended by now. "You don't have to pay me. I'd enjoy it."

"I prefer to keep this on a professional basis."

Sherry yielded. "If you insist, put me on the clock for two hours. After that, sticking around will be my choice, okay?"

He agreed. "This ought to cheer up the kids. They're disappointed about Oliver and Brooke. Pick you up in ten minutes?"

"I'll be ready."

She rang off with a shiver of anticipation. Partly for seeing the children but, Sherry had to admit, for seeing their uncle, too.

Chapter Eight

Rafe had never seen the amusement center lot so full. "Must be a private party," he said while waiting for a sport-utility vehicle to vacate a space.

"There was a charity tournament earlier," Sherry informed him. "I read about it in the paper. I thought they'd have left already."

Wearing a white sailor top with matching blue shorts, she looked too perky for words. Perkiness was not a quality that generally appealed to Rafe, but Sherry pulled it off. He tried not to notice the fullness of her lips or the radiance of her skin. She worked for him, which meant she was off-limits.

He'd been anticipating a rough time after Oliver called to say Brooke was too tired to join them today, forcing them to beg off. The children's disappointment had sunk the entire house in gloom, but news of Sherry's participation had revived their spirits. Juan had hurried to change out of his grubby play clothes, and when Rafe brushed Sofia's tangled hair, she'd winced rather than screeched at the tugs.

The four of them now strolled toward the arcade

building that fronted the miniature-golf course. Juan held Sherry's hand, skipping in place but not pulling free as he often did. At Rafe's side, Sofia tried to mimic Sherry's graceful gait.

His niece was outgrowing her shorts and T-shirts, Rafe noted. Juan could also use new clothes before school started. Since Rafe had no idea what to pick for them, he hoped his new nanny would tackle the job.

In the dim interior, the clanging of arcade games and the flash of lights assaulted his senses. Teens and preteens clustered around stations, cheering for competitors and demanding their turns. While Juan wanted to hang back and watch, Rafe shepherded his band through the maze.

Via a rear door, they emerged once again into dazzling daylight. Beyond the check-in area swarming with guests, the course resembled a miniature fairyland, with a windmill, a castle and a coiled dragon among the obstacles.

Instead of the usual assortment of scruffy teens and families in shorts, Rafe noted a number of middle-aged executive types in sharp clothes. Even their shoes looked expensive. As for the children's attire, either someone had starched and ironed those outfits or they were new.

A couple of people nodded politely toward Sherry and a few shot them curious glances, but nobody stopped to talk. Apparently, these were what passed for old friends among the snooty class.

"What did you say about a charity tournament?" Rafe asked.

She cleared her throat. "It was scheduled for noon, and I'd hoped it would be over already."

From nearby, an apron-clad employee interjected.

"The automatic scoring system malfunctioned. They didn't begin until an hour ago."

"Two hours overdue? I'm surprised they waited that long," Rafe said.

"The organizers served free snacks and gave free tokens for the arcade games." The attendant caught sight of a man in designer casuals gesturing imperiously. "Excuse me."

"Thanks for the info," Rafe said, then turned to Sherry. "Two hours is a long time to wait."

"Oh, most of them probably got here at least an hour late, anyway." She shrugged. "That's just the way they are."

"Unc' Rafe!" Sofia, who'd been staring in dismay at the forest of people, raised her arms.

He scooped her up. "I hope they get done soon." Although the money went to a good cause, he felt an irrational resentment of these well-heeled folks for taking over a popular family activity on a Saturday.

"Let's start," Juan said.

"Any reason we can't?" Rafe asked.

Sherry regarded the cashier's window. "They've posted special prices for the event. Those look expensive."

Sure enough, the cost had quadrupled. "I'd rather donate directly to my favorite charities. Why don't we play arcade games instead?"

Juan seconded the notion enthusiastically.

Rafe didn't expect the prospect of lingering in that noisy interior to appeal to Sherry. Nevertheless, she acquiesced. "Sure, why not?"

She started to turn back toward the building, then stopped to stare at a pair of women. Rafe didn't recognize the shorter one, a thirtyish lady with honey-brown hair, but the lean figure with dramatically upswept red hair was Helen Salonica. Her husband, Nicholas, owned the Smile Central orthodontist's office where Brooke had worked. The Salonicas had lost an initial investment with Winston, and according to Brooke, narrowly avoided making a second investment that would have bankrupted them when he disappeared.

When Helen caught sight of Sherry, she averted her face angrily. The other woman hesitated, as if considering whether to say hello, but a balding man took her arm and the moment passed.

"Who's that?" Rafe asked. "Not Helen. Her friend."

"Becky Rosen. I told you about her and her stepfather." Sherry released a long breath. "We used to be close."

Although until recently Rafe had been one of Sherry's sharpest critics, he experienced a pang of dislike for these faithless chums. Wasn't losing her fiancé and being reduced to near poverty enough of a punishment for any harm she'd accidentally wrought? "Let's get moving."

She accompanied him without comment. Her mouth remained pressed into a thin line, though, and her usual sparkle had dimmed.

"Those people must trip over their feet a lot," Rafe said to cheer her up.

She blinked. "Why?"

"It's hard to see with your nose in the air."

She laughed. "They aren't all snobs."

"Coulda fooled me." He selected a child-appropriate game and found footstools for the twins. The kids got the hang of the controls remarkably fast.

Sofia lost interest before Juan. She and Sherry wandered off to get drinks from the snack bar. A short while later, from the next aisle, Rafe heard a young male voice shout, "It's her! That heiress."

"Leave us alone." He could barely make out Sherry's words over the buzz of noise.

"Look this way!" The loudmouth had no trouble making himself heard.

"Smile at me, Sherry baby!" demanded a second youth.

"Hey, let's call the radio station," someone said.

Rafe interrupted Juan's game. "Sorry, son, but here's our chance to be knights in shining armor," he told the startled boy, and whisked him around a bank of arcade games.

A chunky youth of about sixteen was blocking Sherry and Sofia's escape, while his friend snapped their pictures. Sherry had her arms around the girl, trying to keep her out of the photographs.

Rage blurred Rafe's vision, and he had to restrain himself as he yanked the youth out of the way. "I could have you both arrested," he snapped. "You're terrorizing my daughter."

The other kid, who appeared slightly younger, paled visibly. "We're just taking pictures."

Rafe snatched his phone and deleted the shots. "Restraining a person against her will is a crime."

"Shame on you both," Sherry interjected. "Are your parents here?"

They both shook their heads. When Rafe returned the phone, the younger boy tucked it in his pocket. "I figured it was okay, since she's famous. People do it all the time on television."

"People do a lot of stupid things on television," Sherry told them.

Finally, they looked ashamed. "We're sorry."

No point lecturing them further, Rafe decided. With luck, these kids got the point.

Sofia grabbed his hand as they left. "They were mean."

"Are you okay?" he asked.

"Yeah. I wasn't scared. Just mad."

"You should punch them," Juan announced to his uncle.

Although Rafe agreed, he knew it wasn't the right reaction. "If I did that, I'd be acting like a criminal," he responded. "For one thing, they're smaller than me. Also, we don't fight unless it's absolutely necessary, like to protect ourselves."

His nephew frowned. "Why not?"

"Because that only makes things worse. You get better results with diplomacy," Rafe said.

"That's right," Sherry agreed. "They didn't mean us any harm. All the same, I'm glad you were there."

"So am I." Rafe unlocked the car. As they fastened the children into their booster seats, he murmured, "I'm not sure what to suggest if this happens when you're out alone with the kids."

"If I can't find a way to leave, I'll call the police," she replied. "There are limits to what I'll tolerate."

Her chin rose. This lady was tougher than she looked.

As he drove home, Rafe turned on the radio in search of soothing music. He should have paid more attention to the station because without warning the voice of Deejay V.J. broke in to say, "Folks, I'm sure those of you following the trials and tribulations of Orange County's poor little rich girl will be thrilled to hear that we've had a new Sherry sighting.

"Our favorite heiress put in a visit to the Children's Fund Miniature Golf Tournament. According to our source, she brought her handsome chauffeur, or is he her bodyguard? If anybody has the answer, I'd like to give you a gift certificate."

Rafe switched it off. "My apologies."

"What's a Sherry sighting?" Sofia asked.

"A stupid contest the radio's running," Sherry said over her shoulder. "I don't understand why they think I'm that interesting."

"Are you really famous?" Juan asked.

"Only to silly locals who lead boring lives."

"Well put." Rafe couldn't help seeing the amusing side, though. "At least they described me as handsome."

"Well, you are." Her smile cheered him. "But let's hope none of your neighbors tattle on you."

He was confident on that score. "They won't. Remember when a photographer showed up right after you moved in?"

Sherry nodded. "That had me worried. I'm delighted he stopped, although I've never been sure why he didn't come back."

"He ran into a few problems."

"What kind of problems?"

Rafe had heard the story from Maryam. "When he sneaked through Minnie's yard, she saw him out the window and turned on her sprinklers. Then he moved across the street and tried to hide in the Chings' bushes. Suzy Ching let her dog chase him down the block."

"And that was the end of it?"

"I guess he got the message."

"The neighbors are wonderful." Sherry sighed. "I wish we hadn't gotten off on the wrong foot."

So did Rafe. "They're a great group."

In the rear seat, the children were dozing. The rhythm of the car acted better than a sleeping pill, he reflected.

"That reminds me, I met a woman today. Renée Trent," Sherry said. "She seems like a nice person."

"She is. I've run into her a couple of times."

"She's gorgeous." Sherry didn't sound envious, but as if she was just stating a fact.

"Very glamorous." Rafe had noticed the stunning blond hairdresser when she'd moved in the previous year, of course, but hadn't considered asking her out. There had been no chemistry. Besides, Oliver had dated her for a while before falling for Brooke.

They halted in front of Sherry's bungalow. "I appreciate your help today," he said.

She seemed to be in no hurry to leave. Behind them, the children had fallen asleep. "What're you guys doing for dinner?"

"Ordering pizza."

"That sounds like fun."

"You can join us if you want," Rafe told her. "My treat."

"I'd like that." Her eyes glimmered. "I haven't had this much fun in a long time."

"We didn't do much. Mostly stood around the arcade and lectured underage photo fiends."

"Yes, but...well, you've made me feel like part of a family. Thank you."

He didn't know how to respond, so he simply hit the gas and zipped across to his driveway.

A few minutes later, the kids, refreshed by their nap, gathered around the kitchen phone.

"I want pepperoni," Juan volunteered.

"Onions," said Sofia.

"What about you?" Rafe asked Sherry.

"I-I'm not sure."

"You don't have a favorite?" He hoped the local place stocked whatever it was. Chances were she was accustomed to the unusual toppings typically served at high-end restaurants.

Her cheeks grew pink. "Elliott always ordered anchovies."

"He never asked what you wanted?" Rafe couldn't believe a man as socially adept as her ex-husband had been that much of a boor.

"At first he did," Sherry conceded. "I told him whatever he chose would be fine."

"You were married how long?"

"Seven years."

For seven years that oaf of a husband had never wondered what his wife liked. And she'd gone along with being treated like a nonentity. "Don't ever do that with me," Rafe said. "If you want something, or even suspect you might want something, speak up."

Her eyes grew round. "I—I think I'd like sun-dried tomatoes. Does that sound pretentious?"

"It sounds tasty." He pulled a coupon from the drawer. "This includes three toppings, so we're set." He handed it to her.

"Don't you have a favorite?"

"I like everything. And I'm *not* just being polite," he said.

Beneath their gazes, she made the call and ordered

the pizza. At the children's urging and with Rafe's consent, she added cinnamon rolls for dessert.

Afterward, Juan tugged on her blouse. "Come play with me."

"Well…"

"No, me!" Sofia demanded. "I'll show you my dolls."

Rafe raised his hands for silence. "Sherry's my guest tonight, not your playmate. That reminds me—we missed quiet time today. To your rooms, guys, until dinner arrives."

"Dad!" Sofia protested.

"We'll let you know when the pizza gets here." Not until she and Juan had gone off to their rooms did Rafe realize what had happened. "She called me Dad!"

"That's wonderful!" Sherry exclaimed. "It's a real breakthrough."

"It sure is." Despite his weariness, Rafe felt like he was floating.

"What do they usually do during quiet time?" she asked when the children had vanished.

"It's a chance for everyone to relax. They flip through picture books or play with toys," he explained. "No electronic devices. They entertain themselves."

"Where'd you learn so much?" she asked, following him into the living room.

"Mostly from my aunt Angela." Oliver's mother, who lived a fifteen-minute drive away, had seized the initiative in coaching Rafe, while his parents grieved and coped with the heart attack his grandmother had suffered on hearing the news.

"You're lucky to have such a big family," Sherry said wistfully.

"Don't you have relatives? What about your grandparents?" Rafe's family might not be rich, but they made up for that in enthusiasm.

"Dad's folks died young, and my mom refused to let hers near me. She described them as abusive." After the boating accident, Sherry told him, she'd let Elliott, as the family lawyer, notify her grandmother. The woman's response had been to demand a share of the inheritance.

"Unbelievable." It was hard to picture this sweet young woman with such a grasping relative.

"He set her straight about that," she continued. "I was only nineteen and incredibly sheltered. I don't know what I'd have done without Elliott."

The man had protected Sherry from everyone but himself, Rafe thought. He could see how, left alone in the world, she'd relied on her trusted adviser—more than he deserved. "What about aunts, uncles and cousins?"

"Dad was an only child. Mom and her sister loathed each other. I guess my aunt was a lot like my grandma."

"So you had a lonely childhood." He'd assumed most people marked holidays and birthdays with large family gatherings. Obviously that wasn't true for Sherry.

"Actually, my mom and dad showered me with attention. I was never alone with them around." Sherry circled the living room, examining the framed landscapes Rafe's brother, an avid amateur photographer, had shot on trips to national parks. "I wish they'd taught me to fend for myself, though. It's hard learning to do so at my age."

"You've landed a job, even if it doesn't pay a lot," he

reminded her. "You mentioned meeting Renée, so I presume you're making friends, too."

"I can't believe how nice she was." Sherry lingered in front of a mountain scene from Yosemite. "She offered to cut my hair for free. And Sofia's, too, if that's all right with you."

Rafe shook his head. "My mom trims it every few months. That's enough."

Sherry glanced toward the children's bedrooms. "She'd look awfully cute. I mean, even cuter."

Taking a four-year-old to a beauty shop struck him as overkill. "Our neighbor Diane says at her school she sees students as young as six or seven wearing makeup. She disapproves, and so do I. Preserving kids' innocence is important."

If he expected an argument, he was pleasantly surprised. "You're such a caring dad."

The compliment pleased him. He wasn't naive about how his view might appear, however. "Orange County's a materialistic place. Most people would consider me stern and old-fashioned."

"I wish more parents had your attitude," Sherry said, "but I wish you'd reconsider about Sofia getting a professional haircut."

On the verge of refusing, Rafe decided to hear her out. "Why?"

"First, she might enjoy going with me and having a fuss made over her. Second, girls who're confident about their appearance are less likely to get picked on at school."

This seemed early to worry about peer pressure. Still, Diane had mentioned that young girls could be quite cruel, and growing up without a mother was likely to put Sofia at a disadvantage. "I suppose a simple haircut won't harm anything. Just don't overdo it."

"Of course not. Oh, this'll be so much fun." Her spirits brightened. "She'll be the darling of the salon."

"I appreciate your doing this. She definitely could use a woman's touch." *And so could I,* Rafe mused.

The doorbell rang. "Pizza's here," Sherry said happily.

"Twenty-five minutes. Excellent." Rafe went to pay the deliveryman while she summoned the kids to the table.

The pizza was great. Sherry swore she preferred it to the gourmet variety, although that was probably because she didn't much care for anchovies.

After dinner, at Juan's request, she went back to her place and fetched her guitar. Her sweet soprano soared through old favorites, including "Twinkle, Twinkle Little Star" and "Cielito Lindo," an upbeat Mexican song that, she explained, she'd learned in a Spanish class. The children joined in eagerly.

A wave of nostalgia caught Rafe. "Grandma Corazón used to sing that when I was little."

"She sings it to us, too," Sofia said.

They ran through an extra chorus for good measure. Then Sherry launched into "Do-Re-Mi" from *The Sound of Music.* The children sang with her, missing notes and mispronouncing words, but having a grand time.

Rafe recalled the lyrics from his childhood, the movie having been a favorite of his family's. When Sherry segued to "Edelweiss," he joined in. "A ragged baritone" was how the choral director at his parents' church had categorized Rafe. In this quiet room, however, he heard a new mellowness as their voices blended.

Juan and Sofia listened, faces aglow. Warmth flowed from Sherry, enveloping everyone. For that moment, to Rafe, they really felt like a family.

A few songs later, she set the guitar aside. Together, they put the children to bed, and then she left.

It had been an amazing day. Rafe tried not to think about the earlier scene at the miniature-golf course and the wealthy people whose world Sherry belonged in. For tonight, she'd brought joy to his modest home, and he was grateful.

Chapter Nine

For Sherry, the next week and a half flew by. Supervising children required more energy and patience than she'd expected, but it was exhilarating, too.

Although Juan misbehaved occasionally, he gradually grew calmer, and Sofia stopped clinging so much. "You're doing a fine job," Rafe told Sherry, which would have pleased her more if it hadn't been the most personal statement he'd uttered since the day of the golf outing.

Business was brisk at the garage. Perhaps that explained Rafe's air of reserve, but still it troubled her. That night, she'd sensed a deepening friendship different from anything she'd experienced with a man before. Yet since then he'd behaved like a benevolent employer, period.

Well, she appreciated having a job, and what a thrill to receive a paycheck, the first she'd ever earned. She tried not to dwell on the fact that the amount barely made a dent in her bills.

As the days passed, Sherry settled into a rhythm with her charges that included meals, constructive play sessions and reading. There were also trips to the swim-

ming pool and community playground, and occasional visits to Maryam's house to see her children.

While the kids romped with their old friends, Sherry kept the peppery Andrea company and freed Maryam to run errands. The older woman, who'd quit smoking as promised, was encouraged that the worst of her symptoms—partial numbness, poor balance and memory problems—were improving. Thanks to rehab, she'd begun taking a few steps on her own, and hoped to return to her job as an accountant after Christmas.

One Thursday morning, Maryam volunteered to watch Juan while Sherry and Sofia went for their haircuts. The little girl could scarcely contain her excitement.

The Hair Apparent Salon lay in the Archway Center, a five-minute drive from the house. The strip of shops also held Oliver's real estate office and Nicholas Salonica's orthodontist office, along with a sandwich shop and a florist boutique.

As they approached, Sofia stared at the large photos in the window. "Do those pretty ladies work here?"

"They're models. They usually live in New York or Los Angeles." Sherry held the door for the girl. "The salon puts up their pictures to show us the latest styles."

"Will I get the latest style?"

"You'll get one that suits you."

Sofia seemed content with that.

When they entered, familiar perfumed scents settled over them. Salons felt like Sherry's natural habitat, and this one was charming, although much smaller than the Newport Beach spa-salon she used to visit. There, she'd allowed hours for a facial, leg waxing, manicure and pedicure along with hair treatments. But then, she'd often spent whole days in idleness. In retrospect, she realized what a waste of time it had been.

Sofia peered past the reception area to the chairs where stylists attended their customers before a long mirror. She immediately picked out Renée, who was by far the most beautiful woman in the salon. "Is she a model?"

"She's the nice lady who's going to do our hair."

"Cool."

Cool indeed; on Renée, even a smock looked glamorous. Sherry watched as the beautician finished a sixtyish woman's hairdo. The short but sassy effect softened the customer's strong features.

"It's great to see you," Renée told them as she accompanied her client to the receptionist's desk.

"I like this place," the girl announced, with no sign of her old shyness.

After saying goodbye to her customer, Renée took Sofia to a shampoo bowl. "I'm going to be five in July," Sherry heard her say.

"You'll be old enough to go to school then."

"My brother and I are going to start kindergarten." Chattering freely, she asked, "Do you know my new daddy? His name's Rafe."

"Yes, and you've both got beautiful dark eyes." Renée eased the girl back and set to washing her hair.

This visit *had* been a good idea. In a lot of ways, Rafe and his family had been in survival mode since their terrible loss the previous year, Sherry thought. A little frivolity was good for all of them.

The manicurist, who was between clients, broke into her thoughts. "Your daughter's a doll."

"She's not my daughter." No reason to hide their relationship. "I'm her nanny."

"Well, she seems very close to you," the woman commented. "I guess you've been with the family a long time."

Rather than correct her, Sherry said, "Feels that way. I love my job."

"It shows."

She *did* feel fortunate to be a part of this child's life. How precious it was to matter to someone, whether as a member of the family or as a caretaker.

After transferring Sofia to a salon chair, Renée studied her face and damp hair before taking well-chosen snips. The little girl seemed transfixed by the process.

In the reception area, Sherry got absorbed in a fashion magazine displaying the latest fall designer collections. Once, she'd refreshed her wardrobe without regard to the cost. Now the prices made her blanch.

The cessation of the hair dryer roused Sherry. Turning her attention to Sofia, she saw how a deceptively simple cut—slanted bangs and a length that skimmed the collar—transformed a cute ragamuffin into a charming schoolgirl.

The child bounced gleefully. "Can I come here a lot?"

"That's up to your dad." Renée removed the protective cape and lifted her down. "I'd love it if you stopped by my house for a cookie whenever you like. I live right up the street from you and I'm usually home on Sundays."

"Okay!"

The manicurist joined in complimenting the girl. "While your nanny's having her turn, why don't I do your nails? My next appointment isn't for fifteen minutes." Generously, she added, "It'll be my treat."

"That's very kind. I'm not sure her father would approve, though." Sherry had to be careful not to overstep her bounds. Rafe had made his thoughts clear on today's outing.

"I'll use clear polish."

"Can I?" Sofia begged.

"All right." Surely he wouldn't object to that. "And thank you." Leaving Sofia to the manicurist's supervision, Sherry took a seat at the shampoo station. "You're gifted. That's a great haircut."

"You're going to be my showpiece," the hairdresser assured her. "Let's get started."

What a luxury to be pampered, Sherry thought as Renée washed her hair with deft strokes. The relaxed atmosphere here made Sherry feel more buoyant than an entire afternoon at her old salon.

Once she was seated before a mirror, the stylist combed her hair and went to work with the scissors. "Have the feds made any progress toward catching that louse Wally or Willy or whatever his real name is? If that isn't too sore a subject."

"I don't mind." Sherry was willing to share what little news she had. "An FBI investigator called a few days ago to ask if I'd heard from him. Of course, I haven't."

"The creep wouldn't dare contact you, after what he did!"

"Winston doesn't lack for nerve. He hasn't bothered because there's no profit in it."

"I guess he's the sort of person who calculates every move."

"You got that right."

During their months together, he'd finessed Sherry

into paying for almost all their joint expenses, including the rent on the luxury apartment they'd moved into after her divorce. As she'd commented to the FBI agent, Grey Jones, she'd been surprised by news reports that Winston was believed to have lost millions gambling. "Where'd you get that information? He would never throw money around."

Jones had paused before answering, perhaps weighing how much information to reveal. Finally, he'd said, "We heard from a source that Winston used to have a gambling problem and that he'd relapsed."

"Whoever this 'source' is, he's either misinformed or misleading you," she'd replied. "Winston's too much of a control freak to gamble unless the odds are stacked in his favor."

The agent hadn't replied. Sherry wondered what, if anything, had been the result of their conversation, since she doubted it would lead anywhere. Winston had likely planned his disappearance with his usual thoroughness.

Absorbed in her thoughts, she was surprised when the dryer switched off. Sherry stared at her reflection. Medium-length and slightly layered, her fine blond hair framed her face with new fullness. The hint of curl—how had Renée managed *that?*—seemed to reshape her bone structure, replacing adolescent perkiness with sophistication.

"That's astonishing." None of the big-name hairdressers she'd consulted in her glory days had achieved anything like this. "You could move to Newport or wherever you like and command any price."

Renée dispensed with false modesty. "I've been told that."

"Not that I'm trying to drive you off, but why are you working here?" Sherry asked.

"I've got a comfortable house and friends, and I'd rather be with people who aren't self-absorbed." Renée removed the cape. "Which you definitely aren't, and I'll deck anyone who claims otherwise."

Sherry chuckled at the notion of this elegant woman popping one of her critics in the nose. "You're lucky. You didn't have to lose everything to figure out what matters in this world."

"I've made my share of mistakes," Renée commented as Sherry got up from her chair.

"Where's your camera?"

"Excuse me?"

"Aren't you going to shoot my picture?"

"That's right! I completely forgot. Hold on. Mind if I apply a bit of extra makeup?" Renée reached into a drawer.

"I'm sure I could use it." She wore scarcely any these days.

Renée worked deftly, highlighting Sherry's contours and enlarging her eyes. Then, with the aid of a second hairdresser, she redirected the overhead canister lights and took a series of snaps.

Arriving customers clustered around curiously. Sherry tried not to react as she heard her name being murmured. When a woman produced a cell-phone camera, however, Renée pointed sternly at the client's purse until she put it away.

"We're doing business here," the hairdresser explained. "Mrs. LaSalle's helping the salon."

"Is it okay if I report a Sherry sighting?" the woman asked, unabashed.

"Wait till I leave, okay?" Sherry said. "Then be sure to give the address so customers can find the place."

"Leave my name out of it. The publicity's for the whole salon, not just me or Sherry." Renée passed around her camera so everyone could view the photos. The women agreed on two favorite poses, and Renée let Sofia select the winner.

Sherry liked the way she looked. She seemed less brittle than in the old days, as if she'd become more comfortable in her own skin.

"I'll e-mail you a copy." The stylist accompanied her to the front desk. "Let's set an appointment for next month. It'll be free, too. You've earned it."

Sherry hated to take advantage of the woman's generosity. "Okay, but I'll pay you as soon as I can."

"That's up to you."

Outside, Sofia said, "I'm hungry."

Sherry couldn't believe it was already lunchtime—the morning had gone much too quickly. "Is your stomach growling?" she teased.

Sofia listened solemnly. "Yes. It's real grouchy." Without warning, she cried, "Daddy!"

He was emerging from the sandwich shop alongside Oliver Armstrong. Although both cousins had dark hair, Oliver's blue eyes and fairer complexion intensified the impact of the other man's smoldering dark features.

When Rafe spotted them, Sherry felt the intensity of his gaze sear through her. Then he crouched and called out to Sofia, who pelted merrily toward him.

Sherry strolled in the girl's wake and greeted Oliver politely. As her real estate agent, he'd been one of the few neighbors to stand by her during the controversy over the cottage. He'd also nearly sold his business and invested the money in Winston's scam, then grown suspicious and raised the alarm. Throughout the whole mess, and despite Sherry's high-handedness toward Brooke, he'd remained courteous.

She was relieved to see no sign of his wife. That was an encounter she'd prefer to postpone indefinitely.

"You're gorgeous," Rafe told his niece.

She giggled. "The lady was nice! Can I go back next month?"

"If it gives you this much self-assurance, absolutely." As he arose, his eyes fixed on Sherry. "As for you, I have one word—*wow*."

A tickle of pleasure ran through her. "Renée's a genius."

He reached out and fingered her hair. "It's fantastic."

Her breath caught in her throat as their gazes held. As if suddenly self-conscious, Rafe withdrew his hand.

"Don't stop on my account." Oliver appeared amused. "Hey, guess who's finally free." Looking past them, he called, "We were too hungry to wait. Sorry."

Sherry's skin prickled as she recognized the very pregnant woman emerging from Smile Central. "Sofia and I had better be going. We have to pick up Juan for lunch."

"Perfect timing," Oliver said. "I've been hoping you and Brooke could get better acquainted, and this way she won't have to eat alone."

Have lunch with Brooke? Sherry doubted she'd be able to swallow a bite. "I'm sure she'd prefer peace and quiet, in her condition."

Oliver refused to take the hint. "I'll spring for lunch.

You can bring Juan a sandwich afterward. He loves the tuna fish and cucumber special."

Reaching them, Brooke removed her oversize sunglasses. A few inches taller than Sherry, she seemed dubious about being anywhere near her. "I'm heading home for a nap," she responded after hearing her husband's plan.

Confrontation averted, Sherry thought in relief. Then Sofia said, "Will you fix me eggs, Aunt Brooke? I love your omelets."

"That's more words than I've ever heard you string together at one time," the young woman told her. "And I love your hair!" She grinned at her niece.

"Sherry's a good influence," Rafe said. "She's bringing out a whole new side of my daughter."

The men were pushing them together. In the hopes of avoiding what threatened to become an awkward silence, Sherry said, "Brooke doesn't need to entertain us. She needs her rest."

Sofia wasn't so easily dissuaded. "Please let us come over."

Brooke yielded, although she still didn't look directly at Sherry. "I can't disappoint my little sweetheart. I was going to make an omelet anyway."

"Great." Oliver gave his wife a hug. "Sherry'll pick up Juan while you get started."

"Absolutely." Brooke didn't sound happy about the concession, though.

Sherry hoped this was going to be a very short lunch.

Chapter Ten

Being at Brooke's house proved as awkward as Sherry had feared. Though her hostess conversed animatedly with the children, she addressed only brief, polite remarks to her adult guest.

Search as she might for a topic of mutual interest, Sherry drew a blank. She had no idea what to say about Brooke's pregnancy, especially since the baby wasn't Oliver's. He'd fallen for Brooke, a casual friend, after she broke up with her jerk of a boyfriend, and was obviously in love with her *and* her future child.

Any remark of Sherry's was likely to come across as intrusive or condescending. Still, they had to talk about *something.* Setting the table, she asked, "Have you picked a name for the baby?"

"Marlene, after my mother." At the stove, Brooke folded a large omelet with practiced skill.

Right back to where she'd started, Sherry tried again. "This smells wonderful. Is it your own recipe?"

"It's just eggs, milk and cheese."

Giving up, Sherry peered into the den, where the children had scampered to play with Brooke's collection of stuffed animals. They seemed perfectly content. For once she would almost welcome a spat between them so she'd have an excuse to intervene.

She couldn't undo the past, she decided as she turned away, but she did owe Oliver's wife an apology. Might as well get that out of the way, even though she didn't expect forgiveness.

Taking a deep breath, she spoke quickly before she lost her nerve. "I'm sorry."

Her hostess frowned. "For what?"

"Those awful things I said to you last spring." Sherry rushed on. "I shouldn't have doubted your word about Dr. Salonica. And only an idiot would assume people could switch jobs whenever they like. If it's any comfort, you probably heard about that fiasco at the discount store when I applied for a job there."

Brooke fumbled with her spatula, nearly dropping it. "That was really you? I thought the deejay was putting us on."

Sherry sighed. "All true. People crowded around snapping my picture like I was some kind of freak."

"The handsome bodyguard they're trying to identify—that's Rafe?" Brooke let out a whoop of laughter.

"It's him, all right," Sherry said. "He took pity on me."

"You think that's all there is to it?"

"To what?"

"To you and him."

There was no her and him. "What do you mean?"

"You guys have chemistry. I saw that today when I spotted you." Brooke transferred the eggs to a platter. "I thought we were having a heat wave!"

Sherry had no idea what to say. She was too excited

to speak, anyway. It was wonderful to discover that she hadn't fantasized their bond.

"I wish you could see the expression on your face." Her hostess retrieved milk from the fridge. "Are you in love with him?"

Sherry stared at her. "That's quite a leap."

"Sorry. I'm a bit of a matchmaker." Brooke filled four jelly glasses. "Oops. You did want milk, right?"

"Sure." She swallowed. "I may not know how I feel about Rafe, but I felt terrible about what I'd said to you. I wish I'd apologized ages ago."

"I wasn't mad at you," Brooke told her. "Merely uncomfortable."

"You had every right to chew me out."

"Well, I'm glad we got past *that.*" Brooke went to call the children.

They had a grand time at lunch, spontaneously conducting a preschool geometry lesson by identifying circles in wet glass rings and squares in the brownies they ate for dessert. Afterward, Sherry washed dishes while Brooke stretched out across several chairs. In the den, the children watched a *Sesame Street* video.

"If you want to lie down, please do," Sherry urged.

"I *am* lying down. Besides, I've been dying to get to know you better," Brooke confessed. "Oliver keeps telling me stuff he hears from Rafe. How you're teaching the kids the notes of the scale. Oh, and that you persuaded him to give them an allowance so they could learn to manage money."

"It's only a few dollars a week, but they needed to start." Sherry explained that her own parents had indulged her every wish, doling out money on demand.

"I never learned to set priorities or save for the future. I'd like to teach the kids how to manage their money, in an age-appropriate way, of course."

"I'm surprised you took this job," Brooke said.

"I adore the kids. Plus, considering my lack of job skills, I'm lucky to get hired." Sherry supposed she should be discreet, but Brooke's openness invited confidences. "I got way behind in my bills."

"That fiancé left you completely broke?"

"Utterly, except for the cottage."

Brooke shook her head sympathetically. "Rafe can't be paying much."

"It's a start," Sherry said. "And I'm more or less caught up. Last week I pawned a pair of diamond earrings my mom and dad gave me."

"That had to hurt."

More than she could say. Sherry had tried several tacks before deciding there was no other practical way to obtain several thousand dollars in a hurry. The designer outfits and purses she'd sold on eBay hadn't netted nearly enough to salvage her credit balance. "The pawnshop won't put them up for sale for thirty days. If I recover some of my money, I can redeem them."

"Good luck with that." Brooke glanced at her watch. "Well, I'd better head for the office. My boss is flexible about my lunch break because of the pregnancy, but I don't want to overdo it."

The reference to Dr. Salonica proved more than Sherry could resist. She blurted the question she'd been dying to ask. "How's Helen? She doesn't speak to me anymore, not that I blame her. I've been concerned because the last time we talked she and Nicholas were having problems."

"They seem a lot happier since they attended a marriage renewal weekend at their church." Brooke pressed her palm to her abdomen. "The baby's not happy about my digestive process. I think the rumbling woke her."

Sherry's fingers twitched to feel this miracle. She tucked her hand behind her.

Sensing Sherry's interest, Brooke caught Sherry's palm and placed it against her side. "Go ahead. It's okay."

A hard thrust caught her off guard. "What was *that?*"

"She kicked you. Or maybe she gave you the elbow." Brooke smiled fondly. "She's feisty. My doctor says babies are most active at this stage. Later, they're too big to move around much."

Sherry had a sudden image of an infant with dark, curly hair and penetrating eyes. The little boy had both his father's stubbornness and his warmth, and he lay contentedly in his mother's arms. In *her* arms.

She must be losing her mind.

"Thanks for letting me meet Marlene." Sherry removed her hand. "That was wonderful."

"My pleasure." Getting to her feet, Brooke gave her a hug. "Drop by anytime."

"I will."

Sherry collected the kids and took them home. After spending the day with new friends, she felt more at ease than she had in a long while.

DURING THE NEXT WEEKS, several of Sherry's neighbors paused to chat during her early-morning walks. She got the impression Brooke and Renée had been spreading kind words about her.

As a result, Sherry worked up the nerve to attend a

local potluck lunch on a Saturday in July. The events were held monthly at the Harmony Circle community clubhouse, set on a terrace above the pool. She brought gingerbread men, which she set on the dessert table.

Rafe was swimming with the kids, she noted. She was pleased to see Andrea walking with a cane alongside her daughter, and Sherry stopped to say hello. Then she filled her plate with a colorful array of pasta salads and fruit, plus a freshly grilled hamburger.

Renée beckoned her to a picnic table, where she joined Brooke, Jane McKay and Diane Lorenz. Diane's husband, a contractor, and Oliver were both working, their wives explained.

Diane, who was a teacher, provided tips about preparing the children for kindergarten, such as memorizing their uncle's phone number. "From what I've heard, you're doing a wonderful job with them." With a hint of wariness, she added, "I hope you plan to keep the cottage. It broke my heart to think of seeing it torn down."

"Absolutely," Sherry said. "My original plan was a bit misguided and I've come to love my place."

While she was enjoying the company, Sherry found herself tense a bit at the approach of Alice Watson, a retired school principal and member of the homeowners' board of directors. With her erect carriage and stern manner, the older woman was normally intimidating. Today, however, she positively glowed, as she introduced George Tyler, a man she'd recently reconnected with after losing touch with him half a century earlier.

"He's widowed now. They met up on the Internet," Diane whispered after the couple wandered off hand in hand. "They've been discussing moving in together.

This summer, he introduced her to his daughter and grandchildren."

"I guess you Foxes aren't so ferociously single anymore," Sherry observed.

Diane laughed. "People keep confusing our initials. The *F* stands for *female,* not *ferocious.* As for the *S,* we may have to change that from *single* to..."

"Sexy?" Brooke said.

"Scrumptious," Jane proposed.

"Splendid," Sherry suggested.

"I like that," Diane told her. "Simple and direct."

Sherry basked in the praise. The women's acceptance meant a lot.

Below, at the pool, Rafe's arm muscles bulged as he raised himself from the water onto the concrete lip. Rivulets flowed along his olive skin until he gleamed like an antique gold coin.

Juan and Sofia joined their father, who'd apparently gone for a final swim in the deep end. Beaming down at them, he led the towel-draped youngsters to the changing rooms.

"He's quite a sight, isn't he?" murmured Renée.

"He... Yes."

"Anything going on there?" she asked.

Despite her turbulent emotions, Sherry could truthfully say there wasn't.

He'd continued to keep her at arm's length. Except for their morning and afternoon handoffs and a few compliments about the children's progress, he seemed to deliberately avoid her.

Surely that was a good thing. *Thou shalt not lean on a man.* She hadn't forgotten her new commandment.

With advice from the neighbors, Sherry had started working on her home, making it more comfortable and truly hers. She'd tamed the squeaky hinges on her doors, planted a vegetable patch and installed anti-virus software on her computer. Had Rafe been available, she might have called on him instead of becoming self-sufficient.

Yet when he emerged from the dressing room with the children and strolled across the patio, jeans hugging his long legs and a smile playing around his mouth, it took all Sherry's strength not to dash forward to meet him.

THAT YELLOW SUNDRESS had no right to look so stunning on Sherry. With her hair floating in a mild breeze and her face tilted to catch the sunshine, she looked irresistibly radiant.

Rafe was proud of his restraint, yet a month of playing it cool hadn't dimmed his interest. If anything, the attraction he felt for Sherry had strengthened as he came to know her better.

Ignoring his warnings not to run, his children flew across the concrete. As she crouched to hug her small charges, the other women exchanged approving glances.

"I wouldn't have believed it," said Tess Phipps, a divorce attorney and onetime sharp critic of Sherry's and Winston's arrogance. "Sherry LaSalle, devoted nanny."

"How tactful," murmured Cynthia Lieberman, a psychologist who owned the house next to Tess's. "Could you rub it in a little harder?"

Sherry rose gracefully, a child hanging from each hand. "I deserve it. I was obnoxious."

"I'd like to disagree, but I can't," Tess responded.

Diane leveled a stern look at her. "Once a person's learned her lesson, we should forgive her and move on."

"Spoken like a teacher." Tess didn't seem offended.

"It's been great seeing you all." With the kids' help, Sherry deposited the remains of her lunch in a receptacle. "Excuse me. I have to help these little guys with their plates."

"You're off-duty," Rafe reminded her.

"Tell them that."

She had a point. Juan was jumping up and down, demanding her attention, while Sofia tugged at her dress.

To hell with caution. "Okay, let's go." With a hand on her waist, Rafe steered her through the crowd, despite all the gazes following them. The best part of this event was the chance to spend time with Sherry. "I'll line up at the grill if you'll handle the side dishes."

"Sounds like a plan."

Working as a team, they soon had the kids settled. As Rafe downed his own lunch, he listened to Sofia chattering away about her adventures in the swimming pool. She'd opened up recently, thanks to Sherry. As for Juan, he listened to his sister for several minutes at a stretch, something he never used to have the patience for.

Afterward, they took the children to the play area, where Grace's and Diane's daughters had volunteered to supervise. The girls seized on the kids with delight, and soon they were all whooping down the slide together.

"How about we take a walk?" Rafe indicated a trail that wound past the community tennis courts.

"I'd like that." Sherry's hand swung toward his, but she quickly moved away.

He felt the same instinct to touch her. And the same reluctance to yield to it.

They followed the path past the courts, where a group of teenagers were playing, and headed into a profusion of brush and trees. The strip of land bordering a drainage channel had become a refuge for small animals and native plants.

"You seem to be hitting it off with the Foxes," Rafe said. "They can be a tough bunch."

"They don't hesitate to speak their minds. I like that."

She moved ahead onto a footbridge across the ravine. Trees on the bank obscured the clubhouse and the tennis courts. Except for the murmur of voices and the sound of tennis balls being volleyed back and forth, they might have been far from civilization.

Halting, she closed her eyes and took a deep breath. The air smelled of jasmine, Rafe noted, and the sharp tang of wild plants.

He stopped beside her. The bridge rail felt rough beneath his palms. "You handled Tess's criticism well. All the same, this experience has been a lot tougher than you let on, hasn't it?"

"You mean being an outsider?"

"All of it. You not only lost your money, you were betrayed by the man you intended to marry." Rafe gave voice to a question that had been nagging at him. "Did you love him?"

She blinked in a shaft of light penetrating the foliage overhead. "I thought I did. I can see now that he simply filled a void. I had a bad habit of expecting people to take care of me."

Rafe was surprised by her candidness. She'd matured

tremendously, in a lot of ways. Brooke had told him about Sherry's decision to pawn her earrings. He wished he'd had a chance to see those sparklers dangling from her lobes, which must have been a pretty sight, but he respected her decision to pay off her debts.

"In a sense," she continued, "Winston did me a favor. I'm a much stronger person now."

"Bull!" The word burst out of Rafe.

"What?" She poked him in the ribs, anger in her eyes. "Don't you dare make fun of me!"

"I meant the part about Winston doing you a favor." Rafe caught her wrist to stop the playful assault. "What he did to you stinks. You deserved better."

"That doesn't mean some good can't come of it."

They were face-to-face, alone on the bridge. "I agree." Without allowing himself to rationalize or hesitate any further, he kissed her.

She didn't try to escape. She stepped right into his embrace, her arms winding around his neck, her lips parting beneath his. To Rafe, she felt willing and delicious.

A flick of her tongue against his sent heat shooting through his body. Beneath his hands, her waist felt slender, and his thumbs caressed the lower swell of her breasts. She gasped.

He longed to pull her against him, to cup the curve of her bottom and give in to the desire building within him. But he couldn't forget where they were or how easily someone might stumble upon them. Also, she worked for him, and he had a lot of good reasons for keeping his distance.

Carefully, Rafe drew back. "We have to stop."

She faced him boldly. "Why?"

He searched for a simple explanation. "Because I'm your boss. I can't exploit my position."

"What if I *want* you to exploit it?"

"This may sound old-fashioned, but as my children's nanny, you're off-limits. I can't take advantage of you." A way occurred to him to smooth the transition back to safe ground. "That doesn't mean we can't spend time together, though. In fact, we're overdue for a celebration."

"Of our first kiss?" She chuckled. "Okay. Let's celebrate by doing it again." She stepped toward him.

The blood rose to his cheeks. "I meant the end of your probation. It's been a month."

She blinked. "I forgot I was on probation."

He had, too. What luck that it had popped into his mind at such a convenient moment. "I have an idea what we could do."

"So you just demonstrated. To rapturous approval," she teased.

"Cheeky little thing." And incredibly sweet.

"If you're going to propose the four of us go out for ice cream, let me point out that there's an entire table full of desserts," Sherry said. "Rafe, you don't have to—"

"How do you feel about opera?" he said before she could continue.

She looked startled. "I love it."

"My mechanic, Mario, studies voice at Cal State Fullerton. He offered me tickets to an opera highlights concert next Saturday at noon. Will you go with me?"

"What fun." Sherry appeared thrilled by the idea, which would have bored anyone else Rafe knew. "My friend Becky helps run an opera competition every year and I love hearing the students. They all sound good to me, and a few are truly gifted."

"It's a date." He didn't mean that. "Or rather…"

Sherry saved him the effort of backpedaling. "It's a treat for your nanny. Get her out of the house and show her some darn culture." Grinning, she darted toward the playground.

Rafe strode after her, feeling amused and a tiny bit bewitched.

Chapter Eleven

Sherry couldn't believe her own boldness. Where had she found the nerve to demand a second kiss from Rafe? In the past, she'd always waited for men to come to her.

Every night during the next week, he dominated her dreams. Surrounded her, embraced her, eased her onto the bed…

Then, each morning, she greeted him politely and walked into his house as if nothing had changed.

Sherry had become someone she didn't understand: a woman learning how to stand on her own, yet craving a strong man. How could she tell whether she was falling in love or simply falling into a convenient pattern?

Maybe she'd figure it out at today's concert, she mused the following Saturday as she sat at her vanity, applying light makeup. Aware that college events drew a casual audience, she'd opted for jeans and a blouse. Make that tight-fitting jeans and a low-cut blouse. A girl had to look her best in front of the sexiest man on earth.

Especially when he pretended he didn't want to kiss her again.

Sherry glanced at the antique clock on her dresser—

half an hour to spare. Restlessly she went to check her e-mail, not that she received much these days.

She found mostly spam, plus a newsletter from Clean Start, a youth rehab center that some of her old friends supported. For lack of anything better to do, she opened it.

"Mix-up on Dates for the Carnival," read the headline and underneath: "Please spread the word."

The chief organizer of the charity's annual fund-raising fair had dropped out at the last minute, leaving piles of work undone, the article revealed. Volunteers had struggled to catch up under the direction of Becky Rosen.

That must have been tough, given that she'd arranged the miniature-golf event a month earlier. Sherry wished she'd been there to share the load.

The story went on to say that the publicity team had sent a press release listing the wrong day. They'd cited the carnival as taking place *last* Saturday, before the media even received the notice.

"Our fair raises half our annual budget. We're counting on this year's revenue to support our worthwhile programs," the article concluded. "Please bring your family and tell everyone you know. This event is geared toward preteens and teenagers, and includes demonstrations of the latest high-tech gear, lots of games and great food." The location was a park in Fullerton.

If Sherry had been involved, she would also have phoned reporters to correct the error.

Well, Becky and the rehab center would have to handle this crisis without her, and obviously, they would manage. What an egotist Sherry had been to imagine that Orange County society depended on her. Since her divorce had pushed her to the fringes a year ago, it had moved along quite nicely.

She closed the newsletter and turned off the computer. Why worry about something that no longer involved her? She had lots to do, including the chance to hear a singing mechanic whose boss made her tingle all over.

The chime of the doorbell startled her, even though she'd been expecting it. With a smile, Sherry went to answer.

RAFE HAD REPLAYED his kiss with Sherry until he no longer remembered exactly which parts had actually happened and which he only wished had. There was the moment when he'd retreated before the kiss, maintaining a dignified distance. Okay, that hadn't occurred. Or the alternate scenario in which he kissed Sherry senseless and they ended up in bed… Nope. Not that one, either. Thank goodness.

Well, he'd promised to celebrate her one-month anniversary, and Mario had been thrilled to learn that they were attending. Rafe couldn't change his mind now.

He listened to the doorbell echo inside the cottage, and noted how her flowered curtains seemed to sigh in the summer breeze. With her taste for antiques and simple fabrics, Sherry suited the bungalow perfectly.

When the door opened, warm blue eyes and an effervescent smile sent his thoughts crashing. *Get a grip, man.* "Ready?"

"Sure. You look great."

Uncertain what people wore to concerts these days, he'd opted for slacks and a knit shirt. She'd gone even more casual—and was sexy as hell. "You, too."

Sherry retrieved her purse and locked up. "Who's watching the kids?"

"Brooke and Oliver."

"Good. They'll have fun."

Rafe ushered her into his car and got behind the wheel. "They're making progress memorizing the alphabet. Singing it seems to help, although Juan seems to think there's such a word as *abbissidy.*"

"Instead of A-B-C-D? We'll work on that."

He continued to talk about the kids, a safe topic for discussion. Then Sherry mentioned their upcoming fifth birthday, which was less than two weeks away.

"Would you like me to plan a party?" she asked as they merged onto the freeway.

He attempted a nonchalant tone. "We'll be celebrating at my parents' house in L.A."

Her forehead puckered. "But then they can't invite their friends."

"Family's more important." He explained that the guests would include Brooke and Oliver, along with various relatives. "There'll be plenty of kids." Rafe hoped she'd drop the subject.

"I don't suppose I could come, too, could I?" Sherry asked wistfully. "I don't mean to intrude, but I feel like part of the children's lives."

He could hardly explain how his grandmother was likely to react. Abuela Corazón had strong opinions about rich people, and unfortunately, Rafe had painted an unflattering picture of Sherry during the battle over the cottage. Then there was the anniversary of his brother's and sister-in-law's deaths, which fell the day after the children's birthday. Grief would intensify everyone's emotions.

"I've got a better idea," he improvised. "My family's gathering on the weekend, but the actual birthday is during the week. Let's have a small party with Maryam's kids, plus anyone else the twins would like to invite."

Sherry clasped her hands in her lap. "Okay. That works."

Despite her acquiescence, Rafe suspected the rebuff hurt. Well, being subjected to his grandmother's scorn would hurt a lot worse.

To his relief, their arrival at the university precluded further discussion of the twins' party. Walking from the parking structure to the theater, Sherry gazed with interest at the graceful high-rises and lush landscaping. "I'd love to take classes in child development here," she told him. "As soon as I can afford to."

"You're serious about that?"

She nodded. "I'd like to earn a teaching credential."

"That's a long haul."

"Maybe I'll start with online classes and see how it goes." She didn't sound daunted, however.

At the theater, they settled into comfortable seats among attendees ranging from shaggy-haired students to senior citizens. Rafe wasn't sure what to expect. His only experience with opera had been years ago when his mother took him to see a production of a zarzuela, or Spanish operetta, and he didn't recall much about it except that it had ringing music and a dramatic love story.

When the lights dimmed, Sherry leaned forward eagerly. She must miss this stuff, Rafe realized, and he vowed to take her to the opera more often.

Onstage, a young man and woman flirted with each other. At a cue from the pianist, they launched into a duet in which she rejected his amorous attentions until, at the end, they sauntered off together. Rafe wished he understood Italian.

According to his program, the number came from the opera *Don Giovanni* by Mozart, which Mario had mentioned was about Don Juan. That explained the flirtation.

Several more songs passed, leaving little impression, until Mario stepped into the spotlight. Loud applause greeted his entrance.

"That's him," Rafe whispered.

"He's got fans," Sherry murmured in response.

The stocky mechanic wore a pin-striped suit and seemed a little ill at ease. Then he began to sing. Immediately his stance became more assured and his expression more animated. The richness of his voice blew away the last of Rafe's reservations, transporting him on waves of melody.

Cheers and clapping yanked him down to earth. "Wow," Sherry said. "He's amazing."

Rafe contributed an approving whistle, to which Mario responded with a grin of recognition. Giving his friend a thumbs-up, Rafe asked, "What was that music, anyway?"

"It's from *La Bohème,* my favorite opera."

"Mine, too. As of now."

Mario returned later to sing a duet and a second solo. By his third appearance, the audience began yelling and stomping at the mere sight of him.

Much as Rafe would hate to lose his head mechanic, Mario belonged on the stage. All the guy needed was a break.

After the concert, they ventured backstage, where

they found the tenor in a circle of admirers. He greeted them cheerfully. "Hey, how's your car working, Mrs. LaSalle? I helped fix that sucker, you know."

"You're a terrific mechanic and an even better singer. My name's Sherry." She posed a series of questions, which Mario answered readily. Did he have a manager? No. Was he auditioning for young artists' programs? Couldn't afford the airfare. What was his next step? Sending around a demonstration CD.

"May I have a copy?"

"Gladly." Mario handed her a CD to which he'd affixed his name, e-mail address and phone number.

"I'll see what I can do," she said.

"Much appreciated." He probably didn't expect much, though.

"What do you think you could do for him?" Rafe asked when they were outside.

She tapped her fingers against her purse, where she'd tucked the CD. "Becky, the woman at the miniature-golf course, has a lot of pull with the local opera community."

"I thought she was giving you the cold shoulder."

Sherry's steps quickened. "She was, but right now I suspect she could use another shoulder at the wheel."

"Excuse me?"

She explained about a fund-raising event scheduled for today and the mix-up with its publicity. "Do you remember the phone number of that radio station?"

Suspicion dawned. "You're not going to call Deejay V.J., are you?"

"Might as well put my notoriety to good use."

"You're sure about this?"

"He isn't going to stop, no matter what I do or don't do. So he can make himself useful for a change."

Instead of letting the subject of Sherry die a natural death, the announcer had developed it into a running gag. He'd made much of an anonymous tip about Sherry working as a nanny, although luckily the caller hadn't specified for whom. Then, as the hilarity over that development faded, the FBI had announced unspecified new leads in their search for Winston. The deejay seized on this turn of events by offering prizes for sightings of either Sherry or Winston, whom he referred to as her flimflam fiancé.

The radio at the garage blared the man's nonsense day in and day out. Changing the station didn't help, because either Jeb or Mario would switch it back as soon as Rafe was elbow-deep in a tune-up.

"Unfortunately, their phone number's imprinted in my brain," Rafe admitted, and provided it.

Sherry dialed her cell. "Hi, I'm Sherry LaSalle, and in about twenty minutes, I'm going to be attending the Clean Start Youth Festival." She provided the name of a nearby park. "I'll be doing something outrageous, so don't miss it." She flipped the phone shut.

"Something outrageous?" Rafe admired her nerve. "What?"

"I'll think of something," she replied. "Maybe I'll throw darts at Deejay V.J. for the grief he's caused me."

"Fire away. I certainly won't stop you."

"You're coming?" She paused. "I figured we'd swing by my house and I could get my car."

Rafe didn't intend to let her face Deejay V.J. unprotected. "I wouldn't miss this for the world."

She shrugged. "If you're sure you want to risk being associated with me. Thanks. I could use the support."

They got into the car. "I hope this snobby former friend will appreciate your help," Rafe said.

"She isn't that snobby. And I still consider her a friend."

He didn't see why. "Real friends stick together even if the relationship takes them outside their comfort zone."

Sherry considered that notion as he drove. "Then I guess you're the one real friend I have."

Rafe's chest tightened. He only wished he could count on her to remain *his* friend, because he was starting to care for her more than he'd ever meant to.

One of these days, he conceded reluctantly, the issue might not be him leaving his comfort zone, but watching her return to hers.

SHERRY COULD FEEL RAFE pulling away even though he was sitting right next to her. For no apparent reason, he'd begun scowling.

One day recently, while the women were watching the kids at a playground, Brooke had described Rafe as moody. "He pushes women away. Oliver says he doesn't trust them. You seem closer to him than anyone."

"Only because we share an interest in the children," Sherry had replied.

"That's not the whole story. He lights up when you're around," she'd responded.

He wasn't lighting up now. "You seem angry. Did I say something wrong?" Sherry asked.

"I'm not angry. I'm paying attention to traffic."

She decided to take a risk. "Brooke says you don't trust women."

"What?" He shot her a disbelieving glance. "That came out of nowhere."

"Every time we get within arm's length of each other, you shove me away, and you're doing it again," she pressed. "I know I'm your employee, but I recognize scar tissue when I see it. What was her name?"

His jaw worked. Was he chewing on a denial? "Lindsay," he said at last.

Hoping for a breakthrough, Sherry asked, "Who was she?"

"My girlfriend in high school." He continued staring straight ahead. "She was the star tennis player. I was a boxer, so we had sports in common. We worked out together and shared our dreams."

"She must have been special to you."

"Everyone called her a golden girl. Guess I was a bit starstruck myself." Rafe navigated around a stalled car. "Her family had more money than mine, but she always seemed proud to be with me."

"She certainly should!"

He smiled in spite of himself. "I'll take that as a compliment."

"It is."

"On grad night, she arranged a motel room as a surprise. That was our first time together," he continued. "That fall, I was headed to trade school and she had a tennis scholarship to a state college. We talked about how much we loved each other, and that we belonged together. I hadn't planned to ask her to marry me, but it seemed so right and the words just slipped out. I wasn't trying to rush her. I told her I'd wait until she was ready, however long that took."

Sherry tensed. She already knew she wasn't going to like what he was about to say.

"She stared at me in astonishment. She said, 'You can't be serious. I have no intention of marrying you.'" Strain gave Rafe's voice a gruff quality. "She might as well have shoved me off a cliff. That's how dazed I was."

"What did you say?"

"I don't remember. That was the last time I saw her. I'd never seen it coming, never suspected I was just some guy to kill time with till she went on to her real life."

Sherry doubted the girl had taken Rafe that lightly. Still, she didn't intend to defend someone who'd broken his heart. "I guess because of her, you've assumed all the women you've dated since will hurt you the same way."

"I haven't been comparing them."

Or giving them a chance. Well, Sherry was grateful he'd confided in her because the story explained a lot about his attitude.

Ahead, a couple of cars turned into the half-empty lot at a public park. In the oncoming left-turn lane, several more awaited an opening in traffic.

"I'd say business is picking up," Rafe observed as he sought a space. "Figured out what outrageous thing you're going to do?"

"Afraid not."

They emerged to the thrum of electronic music emanating from oversize speakers. On a small stage, a dance contest was under way, while a trickle of kids and parents wandered between food tables and game booths.

Despite the traffic, the place was far from crowded. However, new arrivals streamed toward a booth selling game tickets, and more cars were pulling in from the street.

"Wonder how many of these people came because of what they heard on the radio?" Rafe said.

"I don't imagine I've made *that* much difference."

Then someone cried the words that, until today, Sherry had dreaded. "There she is!"

She swung around, and onlookers snapped her photo. For once, she didn't mind. Might as well milk this celebrity business, since she'd finally found a use for it.

"I wonder who's with her?" another woman said loudly, and more cameras went into action.

"Would it be rude if I told them to get lost?" Rafe muttered when a small dog trailing a portly woman bared its teeth at him.

"You wouldn't!"

"I guess not. But I could glare at them."

"Here's news—you *are* glaring."

Rafe's effort to paste a pleasant expression on his face only succeeded in creating a grimace. On the plus side, the dog backed away.

Across the fairway, Sherry caught sight of Becky. Her old friend met her gaze with a hint of an emotion that was hard to read.

"What're you going to do?" a girl of about thirteen demanded. "Are you going to let them throw pies at you?"

"No, she isn't," Rafe growled.

Sherry gazed past him to the booth where a young volunteer swathed in a vinyl cape faced a row of meringue-filled paper plates. Traces of goo in her hair testified to the aim of earlier participants, although right now she lacked takers.

A miserable job, but someone had to do it. Sherry

had promised to act outrageous, and this clearly qualified. "Think of all the fun photos people can snap."

"You're kidding, right?"

"No."

Rafe's mouth curved. "You really are a good sport."

"Sure. Besides, I love meringue!"

"Ever done this before?" he inquired.

"There's a first time for everything." Before fear or common sense got the better of her, Sherry quickened her pace toward the booth. "Buy your tickets, folks! Here's your chance to plant one on the heiress."

She'd already made a fool of herself in public. At least this time she'd be doing it intentionally.

Chapter Twelve

Rafe had squared off against some scary-looking boxers in the ring during his youth, and he'd nearly panicked the day he'd arrived home with his niece and nephew and faced the reality that he was now responsible for them. But for Sherry to sit up there in front of friends who'd scorned her, and a thickening crowd of strangers who leaped at the chance to smack her in the face—that took as much guts as he'd ever had.

She didn't just sit there, either. She blew raspberries at the crowd, stuck her thumbs in her ears and wiggled her fingers, and otherwise egged them on.

She also laughed. Pretty soon everyone was laughing with her, as well as throwing meringue pies. By the time she came down from her seat an hour later, folks gathered around not to jeer but to wish her well.

"I hope they catch that fiancé of yours and get your money back," a heavyset woman called.

"I'd like to throw a pie in *that* jerk's face, and not with a paper plate behind it, either," added a teenage boy.

"That went well, don't you think?" Sherry said when Rafe finally managed to pull her aside.

He eyed the white stuff bedecking her cheeks. "You were a hit. Did you see the line at the ticket booth?"

"No. I hope you took a picture."

"That's all this place needs—another idiot shooting photos." He feigned sternness. "Now quit talking so I can scrape this mess off you."

Rafe went to work with a roll of paper towels from his car. As he scrubbed her cheeks and forehead, and did his best to de-gunk her hair, he heard more cameras clicking.

"Go away." He glared at the observers. A few backed off, but most ignored him, so he added, "It'll cost you five dollars a shot."

"Five dollars?" a man growled.

"For charity," Sherry said. "To help troubled teenagers."

The group dispersed. They weren't *that* generous.

Rafe scrubbed until Sherry's face shone pink. Traces of meringue clung to her hair, reminding him of Juan the day he'd treated himself to jelly on toast for breakfast. "I can't remove any more without soap and water."

She pulled off her protective cape. Beneath it, her blouse and jeans were unscathed…and tantalizingly formfitting. "I'll shower as soon as I get home."

An image of her standing naked in a tub sprang into Rafe's head. He did *not* want to dwell on that. "I'll drop you at home."

"Wait. Don't forget our business."

Right. They were here to help Mario's career. "Of course."

They found Becky tallying receipts behind the booths. Wearing her blue volunteer's apron, the attractive young woman carried herself with an air of privilege. Recognizing her type from his days as a valet, he wasn't surprised when she failed to acknowledge his presence.

"Thanks for everything you did," she said stiffly. "We were dying out here."

"How's the attendance now?" Sherry behaved as if she didn't notice her friend's coolness.

"It tripled in the last hour," Becky admitted.

"Glad my notoriety's good for something." Sherry rested her hand on Rafe's arm. "Listen, I'd like you to meet—"

The other woman drew herself up. "You didn't have to bring a bodyguard. Nobody's going to assault you."

Sherry glanced apologetically at Rafe. "He isn't my bodyguard, Becky, he's my friend. And my boss."

"Your boss?" Confusion replaced wariness.

"I assumed the whole world had heard I'm working as a nanny," Sherry said. "This is Rafe Montoya, my neighbor. I'm watching his adorable four-year-old twins."

"Hello." Rafe didn't add that he was pleased to meet her because he refused to lie. Not that he had anything against the woman, except that she'd turned her back on a friend. Okay, maybe he *did* hold that against her.

Becky failed to acknowledge his greeting. "Sherry, I had no idea things were that bad. You didn't lose *all* your money, did you?"

"Pretty much," she said. "Except for the house."

"I mean, working as a *nanny!*" Becky exclaimed.

"She's a good one, too." Rafe kept his tone deadpan. "Fixes peanut-butter sandwiches, takes my kids to the park and gives them baths. They love her."

Becky clasped a fist to her chest, as if stunned that

her friend would perform such duties for someone else's children. "Sherry, you don't have to do that."

"I enjoy it," she answered.

"You can't earn a living changing diapers!"

Diapers? Either the woman was an idiot or she'd missed the part about his kids' ages. Besides, what was undignified about providing day care? Impulsively Rafe asked, "Do you have children?"

"My husband already had three and he considers that enough. It's the one thing I regret." Becky stopped as if she hadn't intended to reveal so much. "Oh, gosh, I'm making a horrible impression, aren't I? What was your name again—Jake?"

"Rafe."

She thrust out her hand, and he shook it. "Pleased to make your acquaintance," she said. Finally a little warmth penetrated her cool exterior.

"Same here." At least the woman was trying to be pleasant. Also, he felt a tug of sympathy for her situation. Apparently she'd married a meal ticket, and was now paying the price of being childless.

Becky returned her attention to Sherry. "I let Abe come between us during the divorce because he's friends with Elliott, but that's old news. Tell me what I can do to help you."

Rafe felt a tug of anxiety. If this woman was as well connected as she appeared, she could arrange to get Sherry a position with more prestige and higher pay. Not that he'd begrudge her the opportunity, but he wasn't ready to lose her.

From her purse, Sherry dug out Mario's CD. "We heard the most fantastic young tenor, a voice student at Cal State.

Mario needs a manager and can't afford to fly to auditions. He's terrific—would you mind listening to this?"

"I'd be glad to." Becky tucked the CD away. "But surely I can do something for you personally."

"I'm paying my bills and learning a lot," Sherry replied. "Honestly, I'm just glad we're on good terms again."

"I miss hanging out with you, but I'm always glad to discover new musical talent." To Rafe, the woman explained, "I once studied voice myself. I'd have loved a career on the stage, but I didn't have enough talent."

"Becky has a beautiful voice," Sherry said loyally.

Another volunteer arrived in search of change for the ticket booth. Becky excused herself, and they all said a friendly farewell.

Walking to the car, Rafe and Sherry stopped repeatedly to pose for snapshots. She insisted on accommodating the requests, since she'd chosen to announce her appearance on the radio.

"Besides, if people are in an upbeat mood, they're more likely to stick around and spend money," she told Rafe.

Somebody *should* have hired her to do public relations, he reflected. Much as he hated to admit it, his nanny was cut out for bigger things.

SHERRY WAS GRATEFUL that Rafe had unwound enough to be civil to Becky, although to her disappointment, he hadn't flashed those killer dimples. Still, he was a knockout and she enjoyed showing him off.

He'd even gone along with the snapshot requests in the end. Although posing for pictures irritated him, he'd seen how well the tactic was paying off for the youth fund.

Mostly she appreciated Rafe's willingness to stand

by her today. She couldn't imagine Elliott or Winston accompanying her to a festival like this, putting up with the fuss and cleaning meringue off her face.

As they turned into Harmony Circle, Sherry faced the truth. This guy was a gem, worth a million flashy yacht-club members who ran Fortune 500 companies and ordered suits from Italy. She loved him, and she'd be the luckiest woman in the world if he ever loved her in return.

That hadn't happened yet, though. She could tell from his responses that he still held too much anger and mistrust in his heart. The incident with Lindsay accounted for some of it, but surely not all. He'd have to tell her the rest when he felt ready.

She only hoped he wouldn't wait too long.

FOR THE NEXT WEEK and a half, Deejay V.J. made much of how Sherry had taken pie in the face. Although he did mention that she'd raised funds for charity, he still focused on her fall from grace with society—and on the identity of her mystery man.

Driving home from work late on a Tuesday evening, after dealing with an emergency repair job, Rafe listened as the announcer trumpeted his latest absurdity. "We've heard rumors that this guy is an FBI agent, a mafioso or a hit man. Here's one you're really not going to believe."

He replayed the message left by a male caller: "I recognized the guy right away. He's my mechanic, Ralph."

Ralph? What a lamebrain.

"First she's a million-dollar nanny and now she's dating a mechanic," cried the deejay. "Honestly, who's going to buy that?"

"Why do I listen to this garbage?" Rafe asked out loud.

He knew the answer. *Because it's addictive.* He couldn't bear not knowing what idiocy the guy was going to broadcast next.

Or, in this case, what truth. Fortunately, the announcer seemed convinced there was no way Sherry could be dating a mechanic.

At home, Rafe found Sherry on the couch, reading to the kids. An enticing smell filled the air. "Sorry I ran late."

"We made burritos for dinner," Juan informed him.

"In the microwave," Sofia added.

Sherry nodded toward the end table, where a cookbook sat beside a pile of children's books. "Thanks to the Brea library."

"Any left for me?"

"Certainly. In the fridge." Sherry addressed the kids. "You guys should get ready for bed. I need to talk to your dad."

"Okay." They departed without an argument. Since they didn't ask what she was going to tell him, Rafe noted, that probably meant they already knew.

"What's going on?" he asked.

"Let me warm up those burritos," she countered, and went into the kitchen. As she removed the food from the fridge, she said, "We hit a road bump in the plans for their party." She'd scheduled a small celebration for Thursday involving cupcakes, the Hughes children and two more kids they'd met at the playground.

"What's wrong?" In the intimacy of the kitchen, Rafe battled an urge to wrap his arms around her.

"The twins' new friends have chicken pox. For some reason, they didn't get vaccinated." Sherry popped a napkin-covered plate of burritos into the microwave. "Then Maryam called to say her brother's family decided to fly out from Detroit. Mostly they're coming to see Andrea, but as long as they're here, they're going to take all her grandchildren to Disneyland."

What rotten timing. "Does it have to be on Thursday?"

"They're trying to beat the weekend crowds." Sherry shrugged. "I promised the twins I'd bake cupcakes and take them to a movie, but they've been out of sorts all day."

"I appreciate your arranging all that, even though it fell apart." How doubly awkward, since she'd been disappointed about missing the family get-together.

The microwave chimed. Luxuriating in the scent of refried beans, cheese and spices, Rafe removed the plate. "Thanks for fixing this."

"No problem." Sherry lifted her purse from the counter. "Anyway, we got bad news from both sides today. When I let slip that I wasn't going to your parents' with you guys on Saturday, the children fussed over that, too. The trip to the library distracted them, but be warned in case they act up at bedtime."

Rafe was too busy eating to do more than nod. He didn't mean to be rude; he was simply overcome by hunger.

"See you tomorrow."

He nodded again.

After she left, emptiness closed around him. He'd never noticed before how much this house needed a woman in it.

That was simply exhaustion talking. Okay, maybe not entirely.

"Daddy?" Juan scampered through the doorway. "Aren't you going to say good-night to us?"

"Sure." Rafe followed the boy. Sometimes he read to each child separately, but tonight both joined him in Juan's room. Childish drawings filled a large bulletin board Sherry had found at a thrift shop, he noticed, and she'd draped a shelf with a bright yellow cloth to display Juan's toy airplanes.

"What shall I read?" He slid onto the bed. "You guys pick something."

Feet planted on the floor, Sofia folded her arms. Juan climbed onto Rafe's lap and stared into his eyes. Neither had brought a book.

"We gotta talk." Juan sounded adorably grown-up.

"Yeah," said his sister.

I'm the subject of an intervention by four-year-olds? Rafe repressed a grin. "Did I do something wrong?"

"We want Sherry at our birthday party," Juan said.

"At Grandma's," Sofia added.

"You get to spend your real birthday with her on Thursday." He struggled to convince himself that that should be adequate. "This weekend, you'll be busy with your grandparents and great-grandma."

Juan glowered. "We won't go."

Sofia stomped her foot for emphasis.

The situation didn't seem funny anymore. "Yes, you will," Rafe told them. "We're all fond of Sherry, but she isn't part of our family."

Sofia's eyes filled with tears. "I love her."

"Me, too." Juan remained anchored to Rafe's lap.

He kissed the boy and set him gently aside. "She's your nanny and my friend, but family's different."

Especially this year. While he'd rather not remind them that this weekend marked the anniversary of their parents' deaths, the subject would weigh heavily on everyone else. The party was as much to distract the adults as to entertain the children. The last thing they needed on such an emotional occasion was to have an outsider present. Even Sherry.

Yet the kids wanted her there, and their feelings mattered. He wished things didn't feel so complicated.

Sofia darted off to her room. Juan slouched under the covers. Feeling as if he'd let them down, Rafe returned to the kitchen.

He was loading the dishwasher when he heard a low snuffling from Sofia's room. His chest tightened when he realized she must be crying.

He went inside and gathered the little girl close. She nestled against him. "I miss my mommy."

"I miss your parents, too." Rafe's voice sounded hoarse. This weekend was going to be tough.

Finally Sofia relaxed. After bringing her a tissue to blow her nose, he tucked her into bed with a kiss. "Night, sweetheart."

"Night, Daddy," she murmured.

He checked on Juan. Surprisingly, the boy had fallen asleep. Worn-out, probably.

Rafe fetched a beer. Then he sat in the living room and let memories roll through him.

High school. One afternoon, off campus, he'd thrashed a bully for repeatedly harassing Manuel. Rafe had feared he might get expelled, but the boy had seen the wisdom of keeping quiet.

Years later, at his brother's wedding, Rafe had stood

at Manuel's side as best man. He would never forget the joy on his brother's face when Cara floated up the aisle.

And then, last July, the phone had rung with the unthinkable news that they were dead. Rafe had gone from disbelief to outrage to a sorrow too deep for words. He'd felt a measure of irrational guilt, too. As a teenager, Rafe had protected Manuel, yet when his brother needed him most, he'd been fifty miles away.

How could Rafe console the children through this weekend's events when he hadn't laid his own grief to rest? He needed to talk to someone, he realized. Someone who understood the children better than he did.

Sherry.

The longing to see her overwhelmed his reservations. Not here, though, where Sofia or Juan might overhear.

Rafe put in a call to Suzy Ching. "Could you come over and babysit for an hour? I'm not sure I'll be gone that long, but I'll pay you for at least an hour."

"Glad to."

The dark-haired thirteen-year-old arrived carrying a book. "The kids are already in bed," he told her. "I'll be across the street." After making sure she had his cell number, Rafe went out. He supposed he ought to call ahead, but decided against giving Sherry the chance to say no.

It hardly seemed fair to dump his anguish on that cheerful spirit simply because she was a good listener. But he didn't feel like discussing this with anyone else, not even Oliver.

As Rafe crossed the street, the cottage glowed like a scene from a storybook. Feeling more like the big bad wolf than a handsome prince, he knocked on the door.

Chapter Thirteen

Kneeling before a coffee table topped by an aluminum-foil-covered baking sheet and several pieces of cardboard, Sherry wished she'd paid more attention in geometry class. Wielding her ruler, pencil and scissors, she tried for the third time to get the dimensions right to create a gingerbread house.

Her mother used to keep templates from year to year, but they'd long ago disappeared, so Sherry had to create her own patterns. How much room to allow for the eaves? Should she cut out windows or draw them with icing?

A rap at the door made her jump, and she peered out the window. Rafe! She couldn't imagine why he'd come, but she was glad.

"What's up?" she asked as soon as she opened the door.

"I'd like your input about…" He glanced at the stuff strewn across the coffee table. "What's this?"

She brushed snippets of cardboard off her jeans. "I decided it would be fun to bake a gingerbread house with the twins. It'll keep them so busy they won't have time to stew about their canceled plans. First I have to build a workable model."

He indicated the wastebasket filled with cutouts. “Having trouble?”

Sherry sighed. “It’s hard to get the dimensions right.”

“How complicated can it be?”

“More than you’d think.” She sank onto the couch.

“Let’s see what we can do.” He settled beside her. “Are you going for a peaked roof?”

“Absolutely. It’s got to be the cutest little cottage they ever saw.”

Rafe slanted her a mischievous smile. “You’re sure you wouldn’t rather build a three-story mansion?”

Sherry gave him a playful shove, but he barely budged. Too solid, she noted appreciatively. “Just for that, you can cut out the whole thing.”

“I plan to.” After a glance at the instructions she’d printed off the Internet, Rafe began measuring a piece with care. She helped steady the table, enjoying the comfortable sense of working side by side, and the occasional brush of his leg against hers.

“Aren’t these traditional at Christmastime?” Rafe asked.

“No reason not to celebrate Christmas in July,” she responded. “By the way, where are the kids?”

“Sleeping, under the watchful eye of Suzy Ching.” He measured another piece. “I’m curious. Does this ever get eaten or is it sort of a museum piece?”

“Everything has to harden, and it probably wouldn’t taste very good. We’ll just enjoy it until it gets past its prime. Besides, who could eat something so pretty?” She didn’t recall what had happened to her childhood constructions. Her mother must have tossed them surreptitiously once Sherry's interest waned. "There'll be leftover dough for cookies, though."

"Better make plenty." He fitted a couple of pieces together. The angles were perfect. "That stuff was delicious."

"You should take some to your parents' place. In fact, take the whole house. I'm sure the kids will want to show it off." She hadn't meant to raise the touchy topic of the party to which she wasn't invited, so she changed the subject. "By the way, what brings you here?"

He continued tracing lines on cardboard, and Sherry waited patiently. Rafe wasn't the glib sort. He'd speak when he was ready.

Finally he paused. "I didn't tell you the whole story about this weekend. My brother and his wife died last year, the day after the kids turned four. This marks the first anniversary."

"I'm sorry." Brooke had told her about the tragedy. "What a blessing that the children were staying with their grandparents during the fire. But I guess this is going to be rough on everyone."

"I'm having more trouble than I expected dealing with this." Rafe released a long breath. "I realize we all need to move on, but…I still feel angry. And guilty."

"Why guilty?" He hadn't been anywhere near the scene, according to Brooke's account.

"I always protected Manuel. I swore never to let anything happen to him." Rafe's eyes seemed even darker and more intense than usual.

"I thought they were killed by a brush fire," Sherry said in confusion. "I don't think there's much you could have done about that."

His jaw worked. “Yes, but they didn’t have to die. Their employers, a banker and his wife, got out that morning. They left Manuel and Cara to load their horses into a truck and drive them to safety.”

“Was there something wrong with that?” Sherry had never experienced a fire firsthand, but growing up in Southern California, she’d watched horrific scenes on the news many times. She’d also smelled the smoke, which was pervasive for miles, and knew how powerful the infernos could be. Still, canyon and hillside dwellers often delayed leaving long enough to pack precious belongings and gather their pets.

“Maybe not, if they’d evacuated as soon as the firefighters told them to.” His hands formed fists. “The Van Horns, however, ordered them to stay as long as possible, wetting down the house and barn. We’ll never know exactly what went wrong, but by the time they tried to drive out with the horse trailer, the wind had changed direction and the fire caught them on the road.”

A shiver ran through Sherry. “How awful.”

“Afterward, the Van Horns got all weepy on camera, saying they’d had no idea the danger was imminent. They put on a big show about setting up a trust fund to pay for the kids’ college education. I wish I could have thrown the money in their faces, but I can’t do that to Juan and Sofia.” Rafe shook his head.

Sherry tried to imagine the scene. The Van Horns had obviously used poor judgment, and they’d done so at the expense of their employees. “I understand why you’re angry, but not why you feel guilty.”

“When my mom told me about the situation, I should have called Manuel and insisted he leave immediately.”

With his head lowered, muscles stood out on Rafe's neck. "I should have done *something*."

It was impossible for her to take away the hurt, but perhaps some reassurance was in order. "Your brother and Cara were adults."

"That's the problem. He grew up too trusting. That was my fault, too," Rafe growled. "He put his faith in those blasted Van Horns. Maybe I shouldn't have protected him so much when we were kids. I was always fending off bullies and speaking up for him. He had this open, friendly attitude toward everyone, including people who didn't deserve it."

Sherry let out a low whistle. "Boy, you can't win."

Rafe regarded her blearily. "What do you mean?"

"First you felt bad because you didn't swoop in and save him. Now you're punishing yourself for saving him too often. Rafe, you're not a superhero. This wasn't your fault."

"Then it was the Van Horns' fault." Bitterness laced his tone. "They've gone right on with their lives. They just had a baby, my mom heard from someone. They probably regret losing the horses more than Manuel and Cara."

So much anger. While his loss had been terrible, Sherry suspected his rage had deeper roots than the fire a year ago. "Those bullies in school. Sounds like Manuel got picked on a lot."

"We both did," Rafe said grimly. "Until I grew strong enough to shut everyone up. We were among the poor kids at our school. Easy targets."

She recalled the story about his girlfriend. "You never knew who you could trust, did you? Lindsay stabbed you in the back."

"And I wanted to marry her. What a chump I was." He flexed his hands. "I never understood how all this kind of tied together in my mind."

"The resentment's been eating away at you," Sherry ventured to say. "I didn't realize I was stepping into a quagmire when I bought this cottage."

Rafe frowned. "What do you mean?"

"I became the rich girl who was pushing you around," she said. "Isn't that so?"

He hovered on the edge of an answer. Was he about to argue, or to reveal the truth?

Instead of giving her a direct response, he explained, "I came here tonight because I'm concerned about the kids. I'm afraid being around my parents and grandma this weekend will dredge up their grief all over again."

"That's better than denying what they went through," Sherry reflected. "I wish you'd let me come with you. I can't help them from a distance."

"Let me think about it." Rafe returned his attention to the little house. "Now, where are the instructions for the roof?"

"On page two."

Working seemed to calm him. Sherry watched as his strong, steady hands cut remarkably straight lines. Soon he'd erected a proportioned structure that fit the foil-covered baking sheet.

"Wonderful." She scraped cardboard remnants into the trash. "I'll bring this to your house tomorrow. We'll have to deconstruct it so we can use the pattern pieces, but that shouldn't be hard."

"The project sounds complicated. You think they can handle it?"

"The kids can shop with me and measure the ingredients," she said. "And help with the cutting. It'll be a great activity for them."

Rafe studied her thoughtfully. "You're good at organizing things."

Everything except my own life. "On their birthday, we can eat gingerbread cookies instead of cupcakes," she improvised. "I think I'll rent *Shrek.* He lives in a cottage, if I remember correctly."

"Sherry..." Uncharacteristically, Rafe hesitated.

She wasn't sure she wanted to hear what he had to say. "If you'd rather I didn't join you on Saturday, that's all right."

"Actually, I think you *should* be there." He stacked the instructions neatly, lined up the pen and pencil and wiped a few shreds of cardboard off the scissors. Cleaning his tools like a good mechanic. "I'm not sure what kind of reception you'll face, though."

That was odd. "Meaning what?"

He looked embarrassed. "During our battle over the cottage, I told my family more about you than I probably should have."

She got the picture. "Did the words *arrogant* and *rich* figure in there?"

He nodded. "Which answers the question you asked me earlier, about whether I lumped you with Lindsay and the Van Horns. Obviously, I did."

She'd been prepared for that, in a way, but not for the possibility that his entire family viewed her as an enemy. "Do you think they hold it against me?"

Rafe grimaced. "I'm not sure I should tell you what my grandmother said when I hired you."

"Now that you've brought it up, you *have* to."

He appeared to be searching for the right words. Had it been that bad?

"She insisted it was a mistake," Rafe conceded. "She said, 'She'll teach my *bisnietos* to turn up their noses at our traditions.' *Bisnietos* is Spanish for great-grandchildren." He hadn't finished. "She claimed you'd turn them into *esnobs*."

Sherry didn't need him to translate that. But if she had become expert at anything, it was changing people's minds about her. "I'll just have to prove that I'm not an *esnob,* won't I?"

A smile broke through the storm clouds. "You see this as a challenge?"

"Sure. Bring on your—what's Spanish for great-grandma?"

"She's my *abuela,* and the children's *bisabuela.*"

Sherry loved the rhythm of the word. "Beece-ah-bway-la. Got it."

"Do you speak Spanish?" he asked.

"I studied it in high school. A few phrases stick in my mind." One of them popped up. "Like *te amo.*" Realizing what she'd confessed, she blushed.

No point in backpedaling, however. That would only increase the awkwardness.

Fortunately, Rafe seemed to accept her statement as a mere exercise in Spanish. "Pretty good accent," he told her. "I'm sure you'll fit in. And I'm glad you're coming."

"So am I."

After he left, the phrase kept playing through her

mind. *Te amo.* Well, she did love her hard-nosed, tenderhearted neighbor. She only hoped his *abuela* wasn't perceptive enough to notice.

SHERRY AND THE CHILDREN spent Wednesday measuring butter and brown sugar and molasses. They also added eggs, fishing out pieces of shell that dropped into the mixing bowl, then grated lemon zest and stirred in flour and spices. They refrigerated the dough until it was firm, cut out the pieces of the house and baked them till they were crisp. Finally, they put the cottage together, finishing it off with icing and candies for decoration.

On Thursday afternoon, she helped celebrate their birthday with chocolate cupcakes. Sherry presented Juan with a storybook about a gingerbread man and Sofia with one about a magic cottage.

The children took turns scrambling onto her lap as they enjoyed a DVD-fest. The hugs and kisses were the best part, for all of them, and Sherry considered the smears of chocolate that ended up on her shirt badges of honor.

Afterward, when Rafe returned from work, he gave the kids more presents—toys they clearly treasured—followed by horsey rides around the living room. As far as Sherry was concerned, you couldn't have bought a better party for a million bucks.

Concerned that Rafe's family would scrutinize the children for any sign of inadequacy on their nanny's part, she took them shopping on Friday. Her bemused boss had approved a modest back-to-school expenditure, so by plying discount coupons and sale ads, Sherry bought them adorable clothes on a budget. Although tempted to freshen her own wardrobe with a charming rose-and-gray sundress, she was determined to stick to what she had in the closet.

She was proud of staying within her credit limit and keeping abreast of her bills this past month. Although she suffered a sense of loss when the grace period lapsed for redeeming her earrings, she hoped the pawnshop wouldn't find a buyer before she managed to scrape together the money.

On Saturday morning, she tried on and rejected three outfits before choosing a pair of crisp denim shorts and an embroidered blouse. Surely the children's great-grandma couldn't find anything *esnobbish* about that.

At Rafe's, the children were overexcited and their father in a stern mood. "You kids need to settle," he grumbled when they darted around, nearly tripping him as he set the gingerbread house in the trunk.

Sherry clapped her hands for attention. "Let's play the alphabet game. We can start now and continue in the car."

"What's that?" Sofia asked.

She'd been teaching them the alphabet as part of their everyday activities. "Like, *G* is for *gingerbread.* We're going to come up with as many words as we can for each letter, the sillier the better. How about *A* is for *abracadabra?*"

"*A* is for *animal,*" Sofia cried.

"*A* is for *arf, arf,*" barked Juan.

The children laughed. Rafe spared Sherry a grateful look. "*A* is for *are you all ready to go?*"

The children nodded eagerly.

"Then let's fetch those backpacks and hit the road."

They darted off toward the house. Remembering that they faced an hour's drive, Sherry called, "*B* is for *bathroom.*"

"*B* is for *beat you there!*" Sofia cried, and raced ahead.

Rafe chuckled. "*B* is for *brilliant,*" he told Sherry.

"As in, you have brilliant children," she replied. While she'd much rather have stood in the driveway enjoying the play of sunlight across Rafe's face and the look of approval in his shining eyes, she turned and followed the kids.

The drive to L.A. passed quickly. When the children tired of the game, Sherry led them in a song. By now, they knew a whole range of tunes.

At last they exited the freeway onto a thoroughfare lined with shops and restaurants. Sherry noted a couple of thrift stores with interesting window displays. Until this summer, she'd have turned up her nose at places like that; now she wished they had time to stop.

Several miles later, they arrived in a quiet neighborhood of bungalow-style houses. "Is this where you grew up?"

"Yep." Rafe indicated a yard where a man was sawing branches from an overgrown tree. "I used to climb that thing. Fell out of it once."

"Did it hurt?" Juan asked.

"I landed right on my butt. It smarted for a week."

The children giggled. "*B* is for *butt!*" Juan proclaimed.

"Which we will *not* point out to the grandparents," Sherry advised.

"Okay."

The curb in front of one house was filled with cars. "I guess we aren't the first to arrive," Rafe observed dryly.

Sherry hadn't expected this many people. "Who else is coming?"

"A few dozen relatives and friends."

Her confidence wavered. Did everyone regard her as an interloper? In a way, they'd be right. Yet she felt she belonged here. Glancing at Rafe, she admitted to herself how deeply she longed to be part of his family.

She'd have to work hard to fit in today. And to disguise her true feelings from a whole lot of people.

RICH COOKING SMELLS and the sound of voices engulfed Rafe when he stepped inside. The place was packed, with cousins spilling across the living room, dining room and, no doubt, the rear patio.

Juan and Sofia shrank toward him as kids clustered around. "What's that?" A boy of about ten pointed to the gingerbread house in Rafe's arms.

"The children made this with our friend Sherry." He'd decided to refer to her that way, since she hadn't come in her official capacity as nanny.

"I'm waiting for my introduction." His father's mellow voice arose from the depths of his favorite armchair. Disabled in a long-ago construction accident, Herman Montoya presided over his household like a benevolent monarch on his throne. "I can't wait to meet this lovely lady."

"Sherry, may I present my father, Herman." Rafe watched with satisfaction as the pair clasped hands and exchanged warm greetings. He'd figured the two would like each other immediately, and he'd been right.

His mother emerged from the kitchen, drying her

hands on her apron. “So this is Sherry. I’ve heard a lot about you from the *niños*. I’m glad to meet you.”

“My pleasure.” Sherry turned toward Nina and bathed her with an effortless, megawatt smile. His mother responded at once, but then, she never had a negative thing to say about anyone.

Aunt Angela, Oliver’s mom, trailed her sister from the kitchen to say hello, as well. Both women exclaimed over the candy-studded house, and cleared space for it amid a pile of gifts on the dining room table. They’d be eating on the patio, as was their custom during parties.

More guests exclaimed over the cottage. Juan and Sofia took pride in pointing out its many delightful features.

Sherry greeted Brooke and Oliver, who introduced her to Oliver’s sister, Melanie, and his brother, Bill. Rafe was glad he’d called ahead to explain about bringing Sherry at the children’s request. Hopefully, his concerns about her reception had been groundless.

Then his grandmother shuffled in from the hallway. Despite the frailty brought on by her eighty-seven years, and the walker she’d used since her heart attack, the small woman blazed with an inner fire. Corazón Chavez had been the center of her daughters’ and grandchildren’s lives for as long as Rafe could remember.

Her laserlike attention seared toward Sherry, the lone blonde in a clutch of brown- and black-haired relatives. The expression on his *abuela*’s face was anything but welcoming.

Maybe he’d done Sherry a disservice by bringing her, Rafe thought. But she was here, and he intended to stand by her.

Chapter Fourteen

Sherry wished she'd grown up in a large, noisy, loving family like this, where no one stood on ceremony. Nina was happy to let her dish up and serve the enchiladas, while Sherry's mother wouldn't have dreamed of letting a guest into the kitchen. And when she pitched in to blindfold the children and guide them as they swung sticks at a donkey-shaped piñata on the patio, everyone acted as if she belonged there.

Everyone except for the children's *bisabuela.*

Corazón Chavez treated Sherry with cool courtesy, but every now and then her lip curled slightly, and she avoided eye contact. When the piñata broke, showering candy onto the deck, Corazón refrained from joining the good-natured laughter.

To Juan and Sofia, their great-grandmother crooned in Spanish. That would have been fine with Sherry, who loved the musicality of the language, except that Corazón's possessive glances made it clear she relished the opportunity to distance them from their nanny.

Yet there was an upside to the situation. Rafe took the role of protector, quietly assisting Sherry and offering explanations as needed. When she hesitated over a plate of *dulce de leche* candy, he murmured, "Caramel."

"My favorite." She selected a piece and thanked the neighbor who'd brought the sweets. Pleased, the woman went to offer her treats to other guests.

Rafe bowed his head close to Sherry's. "Having fun?"

"Yes. Am I fitting in okay?"

"Better than that. My mom commented on how outgoing Sofia's become since I hired you. She said Juan's much calmer, too, although you wouldn't think so at the moment." On the lawn, the little boy was racing about with his cousins, playing soccer.

"He's just letting off steam." She, too, was pleased with the children's behavior.

They were such great kids, so why, instead of appreciating Sherry's influence, was Corazón glaring at her?

She was sure it wasn't only because of her wealthy background. Whenever Rafe appeared at her side, the older woman scowled twice as hard.

"Your *abuela* doesn't approve," she murmured into his ear, "of us."

"Us?" He cocked an eyebrow.

"She thinks there's something going on."

To her embarrassment, he turned to look. Now Corazón knew they'd been discussing her.

Sherry sighed. This was hopeless.

"She'll get over it. Relax. Everyone else likes you." Amused, Rafe headed for the lawn to join the impromptu soccer game.

Sherry retrieved a plastic bag from the kitchen and set about collecting trash. Nina joined her with a bag for recyclables.

"You should rest," Sherry told her. "You must have been cooking all day."

Rafe's mother stayed at her side. "My sister got here early, and she did a lot of the work." After a pause, she commented, "I see the children are calling my son Daddy. You're helping them become a real family."

"Thanks." Sherry was grateful for the praise. "I hope my being here doesn't make your mom uncomfortable."

"Her issues aren't your fault," Nina said. "She isn't used to people from different cultures, but she'll lighten up."

Maybe, but not this afternoon, Sherry thought sadly.

After her hostess moved away, she watched Rafe pilot the ball past Oliver before kicking it sideways to Juan. Thrilled, the little boy booted it into the wastebasket they were using as a goal.

Cheers arose. Rafe swung his son in a circle while Juan shrieked with merriment.

Sherry's heart swelled. She felt incredibly lucky to have become close to this man. She only hoped he wouldn't retreat again, as he had in the past.

She didn't dare glance at Corazón. If the older woman was observing, as Sherry suspected, she couldn't have missed the telltale emotions.

About an hour later, the light began to fade. Juan was whining and flicking cake crumbs at an older boy. Sitting on a glider, Sofia had her nose buried in a teddy bear, ignoring an invitation from her *bisabuela* to come sit on her lap. Exhaustion must be catching up with them.

The shrill of a pitch pipe and the plucking of guitar strings drew her attention to Rafe's father, ensconced in a sturdy seat. "Herman," Nina said in surprise. "You haven't played that in years."

"I'm only tuning it." With a flourish, he extended the instrument toward Sherry. "I understand you play. Take it. Please."

Uncertainly, she glanced at Rafe. From his grin, Sherry suspected he was the mischief maker who'd brought out the guitar in the first place.

Sofia peered at her eagerly. "Sing 'Cielito Lindo.'"

"Only if you promise to join me."

"Me, too." Juan hurried over.

Although she guessed Corazón must be close to the boiling point at such presumption, Sherry accepted the guitar and sat on the glider with a child on either side. Rafe leaned against a support post, watching proudly.

On a chaise longue, Brooke nestled against her husband. Bill held one of his kids on his lap. Everyone waited expectantly.

Sherry shrugged off a trace of nervousness. She and Becky had performed duets as part of the entertainment at Christmas parties and fund-raising events for years. She could handle this.

She began to strum. As she and the children sang the lively tune, the lyrics came straight from Sherry's heart. *"...canta y no llores. Porque cantando se alegran..."* Sing and don't cry, because singing lifts our spirits.

Around her, voices joined in. Some of the onlookers swayed rhythmically, their voices blending. Rafe's baritone cut through, rich and vibrant.

Sherry caught sight of Corazón, with tears streaming down her cheeks. Rafe had said his grandmother used to sing this song to him. She must have sung it to Manuel, too. What bittersweet memories this must stir.

The song ended amid applause. After it faded, Sherry ventured into the only other song she knew in Spanish, "Guantanamera." Juan, Sofia and the guests chorused along.

A new voice joined them. Reedy and tremulous, it nevertheless rang with deep feeling.

Great-grandma Corazón was singing.

Sherry's throat tightened so much she feared she might not be able to continue, but somehow she did.

Tears shone in Nina's eyes, she noticed. And in Angela's and Oliver's. And Rafe's.

Sherry had done him proud. At least, she hoped so.

CHOKED WITH EMOTION, Rafe could barely squeeze out the words of the song. He was grateful for the voices carrying on around him.

When Grandma Corazón began to sing, he'd had a sudden, profound impression of Manuel standing beside her, listening to his grandmother and his children. Rafe could almost see Cara crouching by her *niños,* marveling at how big they'd grown and how much they'd learned.

In all the months since their deaths, Rafe had never been able to picture Manuel and Cara clearly. Whenever he tried, scenes of towering flames and wind-whipped smoke obscured his view.

Now, in their faces, he saw peace and contentment because their children were happy.

He owed this to Sherry.

Rafe knew he'd played his part. He loved the children

and he'd given them a home, but it hadn't been a joyful one until this summer.

As Sherry continued to lead the singing of favorite songs, he remained rooted to the spot, drinking in the expressions on her face. He didn't care who noticed or what they surmised about his thoughts.

At last the sing-along ended. After a final round of cake and flan, people began to leave.

Corazón beckoned to Sherry. With a trace of apprehension, the young woman approached. Rafe hung back, choosing not to interfere.

The matriarch laid a blue-veined hand on Sherry's wrist. "Thank you for opening my heart."

Sherry bent to hug her. When Rafe drew closer, his grandmother said, "Manuel was here tonight. Also Cara. They're at peace."

"I know," he told her.

Sherry glanced up, her eyes moist.

The three of them lingered awhile longer, and then he escorted his *abuela* into the house. In the dining room, where he began collecting the children's toys, his mother approached. "I have a favor to ask."

"Name it." He was glad for a chance to repay her kindness.

"Would you leave the children here tonight? We miss spending time alone with them."

"Of course." That meant another long drive tomorrow, but he didn't mind. "When should I fetch them?"

"Your aunt and uncle are staying, too. They can drop them off on their way to Anaheim." Quickly, she noted, "Don't worry about toothbrushes and that sort of thing. I have plenty."

"Sounds good."

When he told Sherry, she greeted the idea with appreciation. "I wish I'd spent more time with *my* grandparents." Smiling, she added, "On my father's side."

As for Juan and Sofia, they seemed a bit uncertain until Nina promised to fix them waffles. That erased their hesitation.

"You were the life of the party," Rafe told Sherry as they drove along the freeway. "Are you glad you came?"

"It was a privilege."

"It's not quite eight o'clock. Is there anywhere you'd like to go?" He wasn't much of a dancer, but he'd accompany her to a club if she chose. "We rarely get a Saturday night without the kids. It's up to you."

"There's no place like home," Sherry said.

He tried not to appear disappointed. They weren't actually dating, and they'd had a full day. Yet when they reached Brea, he nearly bypassed Harmony Circle and continued on to a point overlooking most of Orange County. From that height, they could enjoy the city lights and see the fireworks that exploded over Disneyland every night.

But the air was growing chilly. If they sat outside, he'd have to fetch a blanket from the trunk and wrap it around their shoulders. Cuddled there with Sherry, he'd start kissing her, and once he started, he doubted he'd stop.

She worked for him, and he had to respect their relationship. But it was damn hard to keep remembering that.

On Harmony Road, Rafe parked in his driveway and accompanied her across the street. "You performed the impossible tonight, you know," he said.

"Winning over your grandma?"

"And healing our wounds."

They traversed her walkway and mounted the porch steps. "I didn't do that. The children did."

"If I argue, will you kiss me to shut me up?" he teased.

She opened her door. "How about if we don't argue and I kiss you anyway?"

All of a sudden, he forgot the reasons why he ought to resist. "That sounds good."

She turned, grasped his shirtfront and tugged him inside. "We'd better not do this in public," she said, and threw her arms around him.

ON TIPTOE, Sherry brushed her lips against Rafe's, tantalizing him for all of a nanosecond before he swept her against him. His kiss was fierce and demanding, a release of pent-up longing that matched her own.

She slid her hands beneath his shirt, enjoying the play of muscles across his back. He brushed her hair from her face, gazed at her hungrily and claimed her mouth with such heat she thought they might fuse into one.

"Don't even think about going home," Sherry teased when they paused for breath.

"I can't think at all." Rafe gave her a wry look. "If I did, I might behave myself."

"Forget that." Taking his wonderfully large hands in hers, she led him to the bedroom.

He didn't hesitate after that. Not when he undid the buttons on her blouse, not when she unzipped his jeans and certainly not when they fell across the bed, reveling in the silken contact of bare skin.

The simple awareness that this was Rafe, her friend and soon-to-be lover, heightened Sherry's sensations to the breaking point. Feeling his lips on her breasts roused such waves of excitement she thought she might climax, and he wasn't even inside her yet.

Then—frustratingly—he stopped. "We need protection."

Oh, that. "I might have a condom somewhere."

Since she hadn't anticipated making love to anyone, let alone Rafe, there was no use checking the bedside table. But Sherry had long ago formed the habit of keeping an overnight case stocked for unexpected pleasure trips, and she hadn't used hers in months.

Talk about a pleasure trip. This beat the heck out of traveling on a yacht or flying to Hawaii.

Once she found what she sought, Rafe helped her slide it onto him. By the time they'd accomplished that, they were more than ready to use it.

They united in a surge of sheer elation.

Making love had never been like this. The difference wasn't a matter of technique. It wasn't even that Sherry felt more cherished by Rafe than by the men she'd married or nearly married.

It was that, with Rafe, she was truly herself. Not trying to please someone but free to release all her energy, all her desire and all her love.

Seized by a raw power that was both hers and Rafe's, she tumbled and spun in a torrent. He gasped and shuddered as a flash of white light raged around them for an endless instant.

When it was spent, they rested in a sweaty, lovely tangle. Whatever might happen in the future, wherever their feelings might guide them, Sherry knew she would always be grateful for this one perfect moment.

Chapter Fifteen

Rafe had never felt so connected to another person. Right now he had everything he wanted. How often did that happen?

They dozed, then made love again, this time more slowly.

Rafe didn't want to set a bad example for the children by sleeping with his girlfriend when they might be discovered, but surely they could be alone occasionally.

This daddy business sure complicated things. Yet, if he hadn't adopted Juan and Sofia, he'd never have gotten together with the woman he'd disliked for so long.

Face it. You always thought she was cute. You just resented her because you'd been hurt in the past.

Today, she'd entered his world and conquered it. What an amazing woman.

In the morning, they showered and Sherry fixed pancakes for breakfast. She looked adorable in an apron.

"I have an idea for what we could do after breakfast," he said.

"Does it involve getting naked?"

"We could try it with our clothes on."

She laughed.

During the next few weeks, Rafe was glad they'd indulged their passion that morning, because he discovered he'd been right. There *weren't* many opportunities for Sherry and him to be intimate once the children returned.

Seeing her every morning and evening wasn't enough. Yet she seemed happy, especially after she attended a potluck dinner with the Foxes. "They're so *nice,*" she enthused the following day. "Cynthia Liebermann was very friendly, and Tess Phipps offered to teach me flower arranging."

The crusty divorce attorney? "I thought she hated you," Rafe blurted.

Sherry chuckled. "Ever since I admitted I acted like an arrogant jerk, we get along great."

How could anyone not love a woman like that?

Aware of his own rough edges, Rafe was determined to do this right, "this" being his proposal. The only way he'd be able to live with Sherry the way he wanted—the way he believed they both wanted—was for them to get married.

He loved her, the children loved her and somewhere during that splendid night together, the words *I love you* had slipped from Sherry's lips.

But a man couldn't simply drop a proposal on a woman as if he were inviting her to dinner. The occasion called for flowers, champagne, a romantic setting and a diamond ring to show how much he loved her.

Rafe began tucking money away in a special account, adding it to funds he'd saved for a rainy day. Researching a locale proved tricky, not just because he didn't want to tip his hand too soon, but also because that annoying deejay was still offering rewards for Sherry sightings. Luckily, Rafe's customers had more discretion than to rat him out, but he wasn't keen on showing his face in public.

Finally, one day, Sherry had had enough of the deejay's harassment. She returned from a park to report that an obnoxious woman had phoned in a moment-by-moment description not only of her, but also, over her objections, of the children.

"I called the radio station," she fumed as she and Rafe set the table for dinner. "I told Deejay V.J. he should stop milking this story and hurting innocent children."

The impact on the kids infuriated Rafe, as well. Nevertheless, he saw a downside to her tactics. "I'm afraid he'll twist your call into more of his lunacy. The guy seems stuck on you, maybe because the public eggs him on."

"Well, they *all* need to get lives!"

The following day at the garage, Jeb and Mario were listening to the station when a recording of Sherry's words started, accusing the deejay of milking her story. The announcer followed this by demanding, "Well, Orange County, do you think we should leave our airhead heiress alone? Is there a statute of limitations on fame?"

"Yes!" Rafe snapped at the oil-smeared radio.

Chortling, the deejay answered a call from a woman named Betty who lived in Santa Ana. "You should leave Mrs. LaSalle alone," she declared. "She's doing honest work, which is more than I can say for you."

The announcer cut her off. "That's one opinion. Now let's hear from John in Tustin. What do you think, John?"

"I'm trying to figure out what would satisfy you. She took pies in the face for charity and now she's struggling to keep her job as a nanny. What's your agenda, anyway?"

"My sentiments exactly," Rafe muttered.

The next caller, to Rafe's disgust, went on a generalized rant against rich people. The fourth, however, suggested the deejay get a real job.

That was the last mention of Sherry on the radio that afternoon. More calls of the same negative nature must have poured in, because the next day the deejay announced, "By popular demand, we want to wish Sherry LaSalle good luck with her new career. To thank her for being such a good sport, we're donating a thousand dollars to the Clean Start youth program. And now, did you hear about the NBA player who's suing a Newport cop for giving him a speeding ticket? Let's hear your opinion about that!"

The guy had found a new target. What a relief.

While Rafe wasn't naive enough to believe the public would leave them both alone from now on, at least the radio wasn't whipping up listeners into a frenzy.

By then, however, the summer was almost over. September brought the start of school, even though Rafe didn't feel ready.

On the twins' first day, he and Sherry outfitted them in new clothes and backpacks and took them to Mariposa Elementary, where, as in many Southern California schools, the rooms opened directly onto outdoor walkways. They joined a stream of children and parents. Video cameras abounded, and Rafe shot his own footage of this rite of passage.

Several people appeared to recognize Sherry, but

were polite enough to not aim their cameras in her direction. While pleased about that, Rafe had concerns regarding the kids, since the other kindergartners seemed a *lot* bigger. Rafe's wariness subsided when he noticed those children were dropping off younger siblings and heading for upper-grade classrooms.

"Who'll pick us up after school?" Sofia clung to Sherry on the edge of the playground.

"What'll we eat for lunch?" demanded her brother.

"I'll pick you up *and* fix lunch," Sherry told them. "I'm still your nanny, just not in the mornings." She'd agreed to stay on from noon till six, and on Saturdays as needed. She'd also applied for a part-time aide position at a preschool in the mornings.

While Rafe had wondered in the past how long he'd be able to keep her, now he hoped it would be forever.

Now that they were lovers, they talked more freely and openly than before. By comparison, he could see the shallowness of his relationship with Lindsay. With Sherry he felt truly himself, and enjoyed discovering new and delightful aspects of her as the days went by.

It hadn't taken long for his mother to figure out that they were a couple. She'd cheered them on, and let him know, as subtly as she could, that she looked forward to the day they welcomed Sherry into the family.

He still hadn't pinned down a date and place for the big day. Every spot he scouted was either too casual, too noisy, or booked months in advance. Also, he was rethinking his decision to buy a ring, since he'd read in the paper that women preferred choosing their own.

Rafe knew he was procrastinating, mostly because of the irrational fear that if he didn't propose perfectly, she might say no. In some ways, he still felt like that gawky teenage valet who'd stood stargazing at the beautiful girl in the velvet dress.

He resolved to nail down the details and just do it. He even considered proposing on the bridge beyond the community clubhouse, since it had such happy memories for him. The sound of tennis players was hardly a replacement for romantic music, though, and heaven help Rafe if a bunch of rowdy teenagers chose the wrong moment to explore the park.

On Monday afternoon, desperate for an objective female opinion, he phoned Brooke. To his surprise, his aunt Angela answered her daughter-in-law's cell phone.

"Rafe? Good timing," she said. "Brooke had her baby a few hours ago! Mother and daughter are doing well."

"Where are they?" He jotted the name of the hospital. "I thought she wasn't due till October."

"Marlene decided to join us three weeks early," his aunt said. "She was obviously ready—she weighs over seven pounds."

"Is that good?" He had no idea.

"It's normal. Her vitals checked out fine."

Rafe recalled that Brooke had been hospitalized once during her pregnancy. "No problems with the placenta?"

"She was able to deliver without surgery. In fact, she only labored for two hours. I wish my first baby had been that quick."

"I'll be over as soon as I finish work," Rafe promised. A new baby in the family was certainly a blessing. Too bad he probably couldn't talk to Brooke alone to sound out his plans.

As matters turned out, however, he got a break. He

reached the maternity ward around five-thirty to learn that his uncle and cousins had just gone to the cafeteria. When he mentioned how excited Sherry had been at the news, Angela volunteered to go sit with the twins so she could visit.

This left only Rafe and Oliver in Brooke's room, where the newborn lay sleeping in a bassinet. Brooke looked tired but radiant. "After eight months, it's wonderful to actually see her," she murmured.

"Ten fingers and ten toes," Oliver added. "Obviously she's a genius."

Marlene really was incredibly cute. "Juan and Sofia will be thrilled to have a cousin right around the corner. How odd to think that, to Marlene, they'll be the big kids," Rafe commented.

"Family is so precious," Brooke said. "Speaking of which, how're things going with you and Sherry?"

Her husband clicked his tongue in mock reproof. "Getting personal, aren't we?"

"Actually…" Rafe was grateful Brooke had raised the subject. "I'm trying to figure out the best way to propose. Please don't say anything to her."

Their eyes bright with curiosity, they promised not to. Rafe posed his questions about finding the right place and buying a diamond.

"Buy the ring," Brooke advised. "She can always exchange it."

"If you can't find the right spot, create your own," Oliver added. "I proposed under the sprinkler."

Rafe remembered hearing that, but he'd figured he'd misunderstood. "How did it happen?"

"I'd told him about a scene on a TV show where this

man proposed while standing in the rain. It was very romantic," Brooke explained.

"I couldn't wait for the weather to cooperate. By then the baby would have been trying on prom dresses," Oliver said. "I arranged for our neighbor to turn on the water, and made my pitch on the front lawn."

"He was adorable," his wife said fondly.

As sweet as it sounded, Rafe didn't think Sherry would be impressed to see him looking like a drowned rat. "As far as I know, she doesn't share that fantasy. I'd like a beautiful setting, preferably with a view."

"Have you checked the Miramar Restaurant?" Brooke asked. "There's a gazebo where you can dine privately. One of Renée's clients celebrated her fifth anniversary there."

"It's high on a hill," Oliver added.

Rafe recalled the night he'd considered whisking Sherry to a point to enjoy the lights. This would certainly encompass *his* fantasy. "I'll call them."

A short while later, the subject of their discussion arrived. Although Brooke and Oliver exchanged knowing glances, they kept mum.

"She's a doll." Sherry sank onto a chair beside the bassinet, her gaze riveted on the baby. "Oh, Brooke, you must be thrilled."

"Also slightly intimidated," the new mother confessed. "I have practically no experience."

"I've never been around babies, either, but I'm sure a lot of things will come naturally, and you can read about the rest," Sherry said. "May I hold her? She seems to be waking up."

"Please do."

Carefully, Sherry lifted the well-wrapped baby and cradled her. With the newborn in her arms, she formed a classic picture that might have been lifted from a Renaissance painting, Rafe thought admiringly.

Later that evening at his house, after Sherry went home and the kids were in bed, he checked out the Miramar on the Internet. It seemed utterly romantic, and the perfect place to propose. He called to reserve the gazebo.

"We're booked for months," the hostess told him.

Rafe felt a jolt of disappointment. He'd been so certain this was the right place. "There isn't a single free night?"

"I'll double-check. Hold on." Computer keys clicked in the background. "Wow, you're a lucky guy. We have a cancellation for this Saturday night at eight. How's that?"

"Perfect." He provided his phone number and credit information. "Is it possible to arrange for a musician?"

"We have a violinist on weekends. We can make sure he stops by."

A cancellation for the very next Saturday and a violinist to boot. That had to be fate.

Rafe took a deep breath. Nothing could stop him now.

"I'M SORRY," the preschool director said over the phone that Friday morning. "You're very personable and your references are glowing, but you simply don't have the credentials we require."

The response puzzled and disappointed Sherry. This was her third rejection in the past week. "You indicated you were willing to waive your requirements for part-timers."

The woman's hesitation told the whole story. Even

before she said, “I’m sorry if I gave that impression,” Sherry guessed the truth.

“It’s because of who I am, isn’t it?” she asked.

“Well…one of the parents saw you here and was afraid your notoriety would affect the school,” the director confessed.

“The radio station’s backed off. Besides, I would be totally dedicated to the kids.” If the residents of Harmony Circle had learned to overlook her notoriety, so could the parents, as long as the school gave her a chance.

“I’m sorry. I can’t afford to rock the boat,” the director told her. “Please try us again next summer. Things might change.”

“I’ll do that.” Sherry hoped that wouldn’t be necessary, though. She planned to put in lots of applications.

But the loss of a potential job wasn’t the only thing bothering her. There was also a much more important matter on her mind.

Stretching her legs along the couch, she sipped a cup of coffee.

When she and Rafe first made love, she’d whispered that she loved him. He hadn’t responded. Since then, while they’d shared laughter and tenderness during their few delicious, stolen trysts, he still hadn’t said the words she longed to hear. Had she scared him off? Or did he simply not feel the same?

He *had* invited her to dinner tomorrow, but he’d done it with such a casual air that it seemed almost an afterthought. She wished he’d give some sign that she meant anywhere near as much to him as he did to her.

When the phone rang, Sherry hoped the preschool

director had changed her mind. Instead, she heard a voice that drove everything else out of her head.

It was Becky.

"I'm such a coward," her old friend said. "I was afraid to call after the way I'd treated you. I nearly e-mailed, but I was too ashamed to do that, either."

"You're calling now," Sherry pointed out.

"Let me say how much I appreciate everything you've done for Clean Start." Becky continued in that vein, acknowledging the radio station's donation in Sherry's name and apologizing for not greeting her at the miniature-golf tournament.

Finally Sherry intervened. "I've missed you."

"I've missed you, too." Relief flooded Becky's voice. "Listen, I'm calling with good news. I played Mario's CD for several influential people and they loved him as much as I do. He went to an audition, and he's just been accepted to a young artists' program in San Francisco. It pays living expenses plus a stipend."

"Fantastic!" Sherry wondered how long Mario had known about this. "I'm surprised Rafe didn't mention it."

"We just got word today." Breathlessly, Becky continued, "I was already planning a gala at my house tomorrow for the winners of a local opera competition, and we've added Mario as an honoree. I hope you and Rafe can join us. I realize it's short notice, but having you there would mean a lot to him. And to me."

"We'd love to." Surely Rafe would rather celebrate his friend's success than eat at a restaurant. "Abe won't object?"

"Things have changed," her friend said cheerfully. "Talking to you at the park made me realize I was afraid

Abe didn't love me for myself. Well, I'm tired of walking on eggs. I told him I want a real marriage between equals, and that includes being able to pick my own friends."

Sherry nearly spilled her coffee. "What did he say to that?"

"He said he wants me to be happy." Becky sounded thrilled. "And he means it, Sherry. He's been much more attentive since then."

The mention of Abe reminded Sherry of a possible snag. "Is Elliott going to be there Saturday night? That could be awkward."

Becky chuckled. "Are you ready for this? Abe decided to stop playing golf with Elliott. Apparently his immature fiancée insists on joining them on the course, and jabbers her head off while they're playing. Abe finds her so annoying, I didn't invite them."

"Perfect." While Sherry wished her ex-husband no harm, she preferred to avoid him. "How formal is it?"

"Some people will wear cocktail dresses and business suits, and some may show up in black tie. I must say, your friend Rafe would look stunning in a tux."

Sherry doubted she could force him into one at gunpoint. "We'll figure out something to wear." They chattered on, getting caught up on the latest news. Sherry was delighted.

After saying goodbye to Becky, she went to her closet and viewed its meager contents. She'd sold most of her designer gowns on the Internet, but had saved a favorite body-hugging silver number. While her old acquaintances had seen it on several occasions, Rafe hadn't. That was good enough for her.

Dropping onto the edge of the bed, she hoped Rafe wouldn't feel ill at ease in Becky and Abe's mansion. He hadn't seemed self-conscious around Becky at the festival. Surely he'd be willing to go to the party for Mario's sake.

The phone rang. Three calls in one morning—that was practically a record for her since Winston had disappeared. Perhaps it was Brooke, who'd arrived home from the hospital three days ago. Sherry had visited twice since then.

"Mrs. LaSalle?" a man asked when she picked up.

Cautiously, she said yes.

"This is Grey Jones with the FBI."

"What's up?" Sherry was surprised to hear from him after so long, but he probably had more questions about Winston.

"I have good news," he said. "Thanks to your tip, we identified several offshore accounts where Mr. Grinnell stashed his money."

Mr. Grinnell. Wally Grinnell was Winston's real name. "Aren't offshore accounts out of reach?" *Wait a minute. What tip?* One question at a time, she decided.

"Normally, yes, but thanks to a little ruse, we persuaded the subject to transfer the funds into the country. The money is now in our custody."

Sherry tried to absorb what that meant. "How much of the money?" she ventured.

"As far as we can tell, almost all of it."

Chapter Sixteen

Sherry must have misheard the agent. They couldn't have recovered nearly all the stolen money. Winston had scammed close to twenty million dollars—half of it Sherry's—but according to initial reports, he'd lost most of it gambling. Even if he hadn't, surely he'd spent a lot living it up wherever he'd taken refuge.

"That isn't possible," she said. "Is it?"

"We believe so." The agent's dry tone implied that the FBI was not in the habit of joking about such matters.

"But his gambling…"

"You told me you didn't believe Mr. Grinnell gambled. If I recall correctly, you described him as too much of a control freak."

"That's true." Was that what he'd meant by a tip? "I'm hoping you at least have him in custody."

"I'm afraid not."

Too bad. Sherry would have liked to have given that loser a piece of her mind. "Please tell me how you found the money." Her brain still refused to believe that she might recover most of her funds. She'd focused too hard, these past months, on being frugal and practical.

Agent Jones sighed. "Because you've been so cooperative, Mrs. LaSalle, I can reveal that your remark about Mr. Grinnell's tightfisted personality led us to question the source who'd mentioned gambling in the first place."

A name leaped to mind. "Ned Newhaven." The accountant at Winston's local office, Ned had acted garrulous and eager to please the authorities after his boss's flight. Perhaps that should have made Sherry suspicious, since the other employees had seemed stunned to the point of numbness. "Why would he lie?"

"Why do people usually lie?"

For love, from fear or because they don't respect the truth. She doubted any of those fit this situation. "For money, I suppose." Angrily, Sherry recalled paying Ned several thousand dollars to compensate for lost wages, despite her own impoverished status. "What exactly were he and Winston up to?"

"I'm afraid I can't tell you that."

Sherry could speculate, though. By following news reports of her ex-fiancé's financial shenanigans, and scouring related articles, she'd absorbed a fair amount about how he operated. "As the accountant, Ned must have helped shift the money offshore in return for a cut. Then he pretended it had been gambled, to throw you off the track."

"As I said, our investigation is confidential." The agent's tight-lipped response told Sherry she was on the right track.

"Luckily, you believed me when I told you Winston wasn't a gambler." Her brain raced into overdrive. "Once you confronted Ned with his lie, I'm guessing he had to cooperate to avoid prosecution. He must have tricked my ex into moving the money so you could seize it. What'd he do, promise to launder it?"

"You're a very intelligent woman, Mrs. LaSalle."

She'd learned earlier that except in a few isolated locales, illegally gotten money couldn't be invested or spent openly. Once laundered through a legitimate business, however—listed as profits from a casino, for instance—it could be used for any number of ventures. Winston might have been a fugitive, but with Ned as his partner, he could have prospered.

A wonderful thought occurred to her. "Does this mean everybody gets their money back? Every single investor?" Her biggest regret had been her inability to repay Helen and her other former friends. Sherry also sympathized with the strangers, many of them elderly, whom Wally had cheated.

"That's what it means." Carefully, Jones added, "I wouldn't go on a spending spree yet. It'll take a while to sort this out and unfreeze the funds."

"Understood." No new gown for the party. Sherry didn't intend to get stuck paying over-limit fees on her credit card again. "But it sounds like you're saying Mr. Grinnell spent hardly anything. I don't see how that's possible. Where is he?"

"I can tell you that part, since it's likely to appear in the press. He's been living on the Caribbean island of Santa Martina."

"Where he claimed to be building a resort," she noted with disgust.

Agent Jones grunted. "As you may be aware, Santa Martina was recently taken over by a military dictator. The country has been in turmoil and we've had trouble getting information. We learned that Mr. Grinnell's been living quite well at the expense of the local government. Apparently he persuaded some low-level officials that he had significant contacts in Washington and could help secure millions of dollars in foreign aid."

Sherry's throat went dry. "How could he get away with that?"

"He can't," the agent said. "The government has stabilized and the people who count are aware of our investigation. Unfortunately, Santa Martina and the United States lack an extradition treaty."

How unfair. "There isn't any chance of bringing him to justice?"

"That depends on your definition of justice."

Sherry detected a note of irony. "What do you mean?"

"I hear Santa Martina's prisons fall somewhat short of resort standards." In a less reserved man, a couple of fast breaths might have passed for laughter.

Sherry let out a whoop. "They threw him in prison!"

"I can promise that we'll be keeping our eyes open in case they ever let him out," Agent Jones assured her. "Thank you for your help, Mrs. LaSalle. I'm not sure we could have done this without you."

"My pleasure." Too bad she couldn't buy the man a bottle of champagne. Instead, she'd celebrate with Rafe.

Sherry couldn't wait to share the good news.

TALK ABOUT ROUGH MORNINGS. Rafe was glad for Mario's big break, but business had been increasing, and the last thing he needed was to lose his best mechanic.

One or two talkative customers had spread word that Rafe was actually the notorious "Ralph." Although the deejay's harassment was a thing of the past, more and more customers arrived seeking tune-ups, repairs and a glimpse of the man who'd been escorting Sherry LaSalle.

Rafe had to admit that, in some ways, he found the situation amusing. Nevertheless, he disliked falling behind in his work. He'd had to postpone some routine maintenance requests until the following week, and that was *before* Mario handed in his notice.

Between oil changes and smog checks, Rafe phoned acquaintances in search of candidates. His best prospect was a pal of Jeb's currently moving from Arizona to Orange County.

Due to the crunch, Rafe worked through his lunch hour, which he'd planned to spend shopping for a ring. Everything else was a go for tomorrow night, however, including a babysitter for the twins.

At this rate, he'd have to work all day Saturday to catch up with the backlog of cars. But he *would* buy a ring before then, as long as the jeweler agreed to let Sherry exchange it if she didn't like it.

Rafe couldn't imagine how Sherry planned special events without becoming a nervous wreck. This was definitely not something he'd want to do again. But then, how often did a man propose?

When his cell phone rang, he wiped his hands before answering. "It's me," Sherry chirped into his ear.

"What's up?"

"Something wonderful," she said. "I'm getting my money back!"

"For what?" Rafe didn't recall her purchasing a defective item, but if she had, certainly the store owed her a refund.

"The FBI caught Winston. Uh, no, they didn't actually catch him—he's in prison on Santa Martina—but they found the money, mine and everybody else's, or most of it! This agent called..." She rushed on, stumbling and backtracking as the story poured out. The con man had been tricked. Sherry was a multimillionaire again, or soon would be.

Rafe battled the irrational fear that she'd just zoomed out of reach of a simple auto mechanic. This summer, he'd seen how much she'd grown and how dearly she cared for the children. And she'd said she loved him.

They belonged together.

"That's great," he told her. "You deserve the best. We can toast your good luck at our dinner tomorrow night."

"That sounds lovely, except we'll have to postpone it. Or maybe we could go tonight— No, the kids are having friends for a sleepover, so that won't work." In her excitement, she was talking a mile a minute. "I'll tell you what. We can celebrate at Becky's house."

He got a funny feeling. "What's she got to do with this?"

"She invited us to a party. Did you hear about Mario?"

"Sure. I'm proud of him." So, after performing one favor, her snooty friend had beckoned, and Sherry was happy to go running. It was unthinkable to postpone his plans—he couldn't get another reservation at the restaurant for months. "Kind of last-minute to call you today about a party tomorrow."

"That's because...well, it's complicated," Sherry said.

"Doesn't sound complicated to me," Rafe muttered. "You get your money back and suddenly she's eager to be friends again."

"Rafe, I understand how it must look, but Becky's not like that. I promised her we'd come. You don't have to wear a tux or anything. A business suit will be fine."

Had it been any other night, he'd have swallowed his objections and yielded. But this was different. "Sherry, tomorrow night's important to me. I need to be alone with you."

"My friend is important to me, too. Please come join us."

How had things fallen apart before he'd even reached the part with the violin and the jeweler's box? "My offer remains open. As for the party, this whole thing rubs me the wrong way."

"You could at least *meet* my friends."

"I thought I already did." A tapping foot warned of a customer impatient to claim her car. "Things are hectic here. I gotta go."

"We'll talk later."

"Fine." They'd straighten this out. Two reasonable people could always find a middle ground.

But as it turned out, they didn't.

The next morning the photographers and TV crews were camped out on Sherry's lawn. Although she'd planned to watch the children, neither she nor Rafe liked to subject the kids to publicity, and Maryam offered to pinch-hit while Rafe worked. Her mom, who was improving daily, seconded the notion.

On the radio, every station was reporting the startling turn of events regarding Winston. Despite Rafe's concern that Deejay V.J. would launch yet another obnoxious contest, the radio announcer congratulated Sherry in a subdued manner. Apparently the scolding he'd received from listeners had made a lasting impression.

Rafe kept hoping she'd call to say she'd changed her mind about this evening, but when the phone rang, it was only customers. The more he reflected, the more he resented Becky's sudden bid to reclaim her. Why couldn't Sherry stay with the people who'd loved her when she was down?

Above all, with the man who loved her more than anyone.

After he called the restaurant and reluctantly canceled the reservation, Rafe supposed he should simply suck it up, go with Sherry and find another time to propose. Deep inside, though, he balked at the notion.

Call it pride. Or possibly realism. Also, what if he lost his temper at the oozing flattery of her false friends? He might do more harm than good to their relationship.

Anyway, he had too much work on his plate to stand around stewing, including a new mechanic to interview. Consideration of tonight's events would have to wait.

THE BEST WAY TO GET RID of the press, Sherry decided, was to give them what they wanted, preferably in a setting that wouldn't inconvenience her neighbors. At her request, Alice and a couple of other Foxes accompanied her to the clubhouse, where they ran crowd control and prioritized interview requests. By late afternoon, sated by photo opportunities and plenty of access, the last of the reporters straggled off.

"You'd better get ready for your party," said Alice, to whom Sherry had explained about Mario and Becky. "Have a great time."

"I can't tell you how much I appreciate this," she told the small group.

"You aren't going to tear down the cottage now that you can afford to, are you?" Cynthia blurted.

The suggestion horrified Sherry. "Certainly not. In fact, I plan to stay here." She couldn't imagine moving away from Rafe and the children.

Her new friends cheered. Sherry's buoyant mood lasted until she arrived home and still hadn't heard from Rafe. His cell phone was out of service, so she left a message with the time when she was leaving.

Retrieving the silvery dress from her closet, she felt a sudden pang of regret. She'd always worn the diamond earrings with this gown. How could she have forgotten to redeem them sooner?

Never mind the hit on her credit bill. Those earrings were infused with her parents' love.

Praying the pawnshop hadn't sold them, she drove to the store, arriving just before the closing hour of six on Saturdays. But although she peered into all the jewelry counters, she didn't see them.

"Excuse me." She presented her receipt to the clerk. "I'd like to redeem these."

The woman checked the computer. "I'm afraid they were sold earlier today. My husband handled the sale."

Sherry's stomach knotted. If she'd only thought of the earrings yesterday! "Can you tell me who bought them? I'd like to make an offer."

"I'm not allowed to do that."

"Could you call the customer yourself? There's a lot of sentimental value involved."

The woman shook her head. "I don't have a phone number for the buyer."

Disappointed, Sherry left. She took no consolation in the fact that, once her funds were restored, she could purchase any earrings she chose. They wouldn't be the ones her parents had given to her.

How frustrating that her money could buy almost anything except what she really wanted.

As she turned onto Harmony Road, Sherry's chest felt heavy. Not so much for the earrings as for Rafe, who still hadn't returned her call. If only he loved her the way she loved him, she'd gladly donate her fortune to charity and be done with it.

Wait a minute—what was she thinking?

She'd always been willing to risk everything for a man who could fill the empty spaces inside her. Even for Elliott or Winston, whom she hadn't loved anywhere near as much as she loved Rafe. In retrospect, she wasn't sure she'd loved them at all. Yet she'd given up her freedom and education to play a subservient role in Elliott's life, and she'd foolishly entrusted that jerk Wally—she *had* to start calling him by his real name—with her money and reputation.

Not that Rafe would take advantage of her. He had more integrity than anyone she'd ever known. But if she had been reading him correctly, he preferred her as a poor woman.

That he *accepted* her as a poor woman, she much appreciated. But to her, wealth wasn't just a balance in the bank or a bunch of jewels or pretty dresses. It gave her peace of mind and the ability to help others. It could pay for her to study child development and become a teacher. It would allow her to travel with Rafe, Juan and Sofia to all sorts of fascinating places.

Sherry would willingly sacrifice every penny if necessary to help someone she cared about, but she was finished giving up her independence to please a man. She had to stand on her own two feet even if it broke her heart.

Which it might very well do.

At home, she dressed for the party, selecting a modest pair of pearl earrings. Staying alert for the phone or the doorbell, she ached for Rafe's presence.

There was no sign of him. At last, unwilling to wait any longer, Sherry got in the car and went to the party.

Chapter Seventeen

Becky and Abe Rosen owned a Tudor-style home in Anaheim Hills with a view across inland Orange County. In the early darkness, the mansion's lights glowed from end to end.

Valets parked the cars, helping guests out of their vehicles with a flourish. Sherry recalled that Rafe had worked a job like this in high school. She wished she'd noticed him then, though at the age of thirteen, she couldn't have done much other than smile at him, maybe.

Flowering plants in giant pots twinkled with tiny lights. The double doors stood open, welcoming guests into a vaulted entry featuring a glittering chandelier and a curving staircase. From within the house, a pianist played soft classical melodies.

A tall woman in a striking black-and-white dress was descending the stairs. Glancing upward, Sherry locked gazes with Helen Salonica. They weren't far from the living room, with its buzz of voices and scent of rich food, but they seemed miles from anyone.

Oh, dear. Sherry would have given a great deal to be clinging to Rafe's strong arm right now. Since the day

Wally fled with Helen's money, the other woman had cut Sherry cold.

To Sherry's embarrassment, her stomach chose that moment to protest its emptiness with a loud growl that echoed in the vaulted chamber.

Helen smiled. "You don't have to snarl at me."

Sherry's cheeks heated. "Nothing personal."

The tall woman descended to her level. "I'm glad we're both getting our money back." With a touch of strain, she added, "I've hated being on the outs with you. It's made life awfully dull."

"Surely not," Sherry said. "You have a ton of friends."

"Not one of them would take a pie in the face," Helen answered ruefully. "Let's go grab a bite to eat and talk about everything we've missed. Unless you'd rather not?"

Sherry supposed that some people might nurse a grudge, but she genuinely liked Helen. A former model, she'd married an orthodontist and been a good mother to their two children. And she'd stuck by Sherry through her divorce. "Don't be silly. Has your daughter decided where she wants to go to college yet? How's Nick Jr. doing?"

They walked to the buffet side by side. Becky hurried over, and more friends gathered to congratulate Sherry.

She loved seeing everyone again. Yet, against all common sense, her gaze kept searching the room for the one person who ought to be there and wasn't. Whenever a tall man approached or a deep voice spoke, she felt a spurt of eagerness followed by keen disappointment.

At the point when she should have been happiest with the course of her life, she wondered if she'd lost what mattered most.

A WHILE later, Sherry was sitting with a small group when Becky approached, frowning. She'd been planning to stage a little concert with the honorees, she explained, but Mario hadn't arrived yet.

"He just called," she said. "Apparently he had to work late at the garage. Can you believe that? It's his last night on the job!"

Perhaps that was why Rafe hadn't phoned. He was too busy earning a living. "Is Mario en route?"

"Yes. He promised to join the singing when he gets here, so I think we'll go ahead and begin. While I talk to the pianist about the arrangements, I wondered if you'd do me a favor."

"Sure." Sherry pushed aside thoughts of Rafe driving wearily home to the twins. "What is it?"

"I can't find Abe. The caterer says she saw him by the pool. He's probably making sure no one left a glass where it might break." A bartender had served cocktails outside earlier. "Would you check out there and tell him we're going to start?"

"No problem." Sherry set down her fruit punch, glad for an errand to keep her busy.

"Thanks. I feel like you're practically my cohostess. You don't mind, do you?"

"Are you kidding? I love it. In fact, I've missed it."

She maneuvered through the living room and den, exchanging greetings as she went. The mood seemed festive, partly because quite a few folks stood to recover money from Wally.

Many had expressed relief at seeing Sherry again. Of course, they could have seen her whenever they liked, but she didn't hold grudges. Her friends had trusted

Wally, thanks to Sherry, and she knew that many of them had lost a lot. When she was married to Elliott, she might have behaved the same way.

French doors connected the den with a terrace. Outside, steps led down to an illuminated pool set among large rocks and ferns. With the overhead lights dimmed, only a green radiance guided Sherry around the now-empty rim.

Beyond the pool, a shadow moved in the nook that held an artificial waterfall. "Abe?" she called. No one answered. Perhaps he hadn't heard her because of the burbling noise.

Although the cascade shone with blue and purple lights, Sherry couldn't see much through the intervening screen of tropical plants. She skirted a pineapple-shaped palm to get a closer look. "Abe? Becky sent me to…"

The tall man was definitely not Abe Rosen. It was…Rafe.

Alone by the waterfall, he was unbelievably handsome in a tuxedo. She had to be dreaming.

Sherry simply stared.

"Speechless?" he said with a wry grin. "That's a first."

"What are you doing here?" she cried, instead of saying all the loving things that she'd have said if she hadn't been so stunned.

"Giving you this." He held out a small red box tied with white ribbon.

Puzzled, Sherry took it. The box didn't weigh much. Jewelry? From Rafe?

Carefully, she opened it. Against a bed of black velvet, her diamond earrings glinted in the light from the waterfall. Breathlessly, she touched them with one finger. “I never thought I’d see these again. Where… How…?”

“I called all the local pawnshops.” His thumb brushed her earlobe, circling the pearl she wore. “I thought you might rather have them than a ring.”

“What ring?”

“The one I was going to give you when you agreed to marry me.”

She was too disoriented to grasp his meaning. “But…you never told me you loved me.”

“I didn’t?”

She shook her head.

“Guess I left that out, huh?” Rafe raised her free hand to his cheek. Utterly smooth—he must have shaved just for her. And rented a tux. How had he managed all of this on such short notice? “Well, I do. I love you more than words can say, but there’s no substitute for actually putting it into words, is there?”

She tried to think clearly, but her thoughts were a jumble. “When you asked me to dinner tonight, you made it sound so casual.”

“I played it a little too cool, I guess. I was trying to surprise you.” He indicated the glorious waterfall and spectacular view beyond. “I wanted everything to be perfect, but this will have to do. Of course, it’s nothing compared to a restaurant in Fullerton. I had a violin player lined up, too.”

“There’s a pianist here,” Sherry said numbly, then started to laugh. “You’re amazing. How’d you arrange this?”

“Mario helped. He told Becky I needed to talk to you privately.” He cleared his throat. “Listen, I especially wanted to give you the earrings because they're like you—flashy and brilliant, but with deep-down value, too. I hope you'll wear them at our wedding. That is, if you're willing to become Mrs. Rafe Montoya."

He was proposing. Really, honest-to-goodness proposing. Sherry's heart got caught in her throat.

"I love you more than anything in the world," he told her. "I think I mentioned that a few minutes ago, but it bears repeating." A note of uncertainty crept in. "You are going to say yes, aren't you?"

Sherry's voice finally got unstuck. "Can we get married now?" she asked. "Can we skip the formalities and make it real right this minute? I don't think I can bear to wait."

He hesitated, as if unsure that he'd heard correctly.

"That was a yes."

Then they were laughing and hugging, which led to kissing, which might have led to a lot more had they not been standing in Becky's backyard. Plus, within the house, a soprano started singing "Mi Chiamano Mimí" from *La Bohème,* signaling that the concert was finally under way.

Sherry tucked her arm through Rafe's and they strolled toward the entrance. "I never had a clue you planned to propose."

"Surprises are supposed to be important."

"Not *that* important." She regarded him curiously. "What changed your mind about attending tonight?"

Rafe let out a sigh. "It hurt that you would break a date that was so important to me to socialize with a friend who hadn't bothered to invite you to her party until you got your money back."

"But that's not the way it happened."

He smiled ruefully. "Please let me finish my apology, sweetheart. Mario called to invite me, too. He explained that Becky decided on Friday to make him guest of honor at her party after he found out about the young artists' program. I realized the timing was just a coincidence. Plus of course you knew I would want to be here for Mario. When we talked, I didn't understand."

She *hadn't* explained very well, Sherry thought. "Becky truly is a nice person."

"Since she helped me out tonight, I'm willing to think the best of her," he conceded. "In fact, I think she enjoyed helping with my surprise for you."

They paused by the glass doors, listening to the lovely singing, but reluctant to rejoin the crowd. "I appreciate your coming tonight, more than I can say," Sherry murmured. "You could have proposed anywhere, really. I would have said yes no matter what. This isn't exactly the most comfortable setting for you."

Rafe shrugged. "I recall expressing the opinion that real friends will step outside their comfort zone for you. That goes double for the person who loves you. By the way, I hope you aren't in *too* much of a hurry to get married. It'll take a while to save enough for a ring."

She rested her head on his shoulder. "Despite what I said, that's okay. While we wait, I can plan a beautiful ceremony. We've already got the most important part."

"Love?" Rafe inquired.

"No, silly. A charming ring bearer and a darling flower girl," she teased. "Do you suppose people would think it odd if we had a gingerbread house instead of a wedding cake?"

"Why not both?"

"Excellent idea."

They strolled inside arm in arm. Anyone glancing at their shining faces—and everyone did—surely saw that they were madly in love.

Sherry couldn't have asked for more.

Celebrate 60 years of pure reading pleasure with Harlequin® Books!

Harlequin Romance® is celebrating by showering you with DIAMOND BRIDES *in February 2009. Six stories that promise to bring a touch of sparkle to your life, with diamond proposals and dazzling weddings, sparkling brides and gorgeous grooms!*

Enjoy a sneak peek at Caroline Anderson's
TWO LITTLE MIRACLES,
available February 2009
from Harlequin Romance®.

'I'VE FOUND HER.'

Max froze.

It was what he'd been waiting for since June, but now—now he was almost afraid to voice the question. His heart stalling, he leaned slowly back in his chair and scoured the investigator's face for clues. 'Where?' he asked, and his voice sounded rough and unused, like a rusty hinge.

'In Suffolk. She's living in a cottage.'

Living. His heart crashed back to life, and he sucked in a long, slow breath. All these months he'd feared—

'Is she well?'

'Yes, she's well.'

He had to force himself to ask the next question. 'Alone?'

The man paused. 'No. The cottage belongs to a man called John Blake. He's working away at the moment, but he comes and goes.'

God. He felt sick. So sick he hardly registered the next few words, but then gradually they sank in. 'She's got *what?'*

'Babies. Twin girls. They're eight months old.'

'Eight—?' he echoed under his breath. 'They must be his.'

He was thinking out loud, but the P.I. heard and corrected him.

'Apparently not. I gather they're hers. She's been there since mid-January last year, and they were born during the summer—June, the woman in the post office thought. She was more than helpful. I think there's been a certain amount of speculation about their relationship.'

He'd just bet there had. God, he was going to kill her. Or Blake. Maybe both of them.

'Of course, looking at the dates, she was presumably pregnant when she left you, so they could be yours, or she could have been having an affair with this Blake character before…'

He glared at the unfortunate P.I. 'Just stick to your job. I can do the math,' he snapped, swallowing the unpalatable possibility that she'd been unfaithful to him before she'd left. 'Where is she? I want the address.'

'It's all in here,' the man said, sliding a large envelope across the desk to him. 'With my invoice.'

'I'll get it seen to. Thank you.'

'If there's anything else you need, Mr Gallagher, any further information—'

'I'll be in touch.'

'The woman in the post office told me Blake was away at the moment, if that helps,' he added quietly, and opened the door.

Max stared down at the envelope, hardly daring to open it, but when the door clicked softly shut behind the

P.I., he eased up the flap, tipped it and felt his breath jam in his throat as the photos spilled out over the desk.

Oh, lord, she looked gorgeous. Different, though. It took him a moment to recognise her, because she'd grown her hair, and it was tied back in a ponytail, making her look younger and somehow freer. The blond highlights were gone, and it was back to its natural soft golden-brown, with a little curl in the end of the ponytail that he wanted to thread his finger through and tug, just gently, to draw her back to him.

Crazy. She'd put on a little weight, but it suited her. She looked well and happy and beautiful, but oddly, considering how desperate he'd been for news of her for the past year—one year, three weeks and two days, to be exact—it wasn't only Julia who held his attention after the initial shock. It was the babies sitting side by side in a supermarket trolley. Two identical and absolutely beautiful little girls.

* * * * *

When Max Gallagher hires a P.I. to find his estranged wife, Julia, he discovers she's not alone—she has twin baby girls, and they might be his. Now workaholic Max has just two weeks to prove that he can be a wonderful husband and father to the family he wants to treasure.

Look for TWO LITTLE MIRACLES
by Caroline Anderson,
available February 2009
from Harlequin Romance®.

Inside ROMANCE

Stay up-to-date on all your romance reading news!

The Inside Romance newsletter is a FREE quarterly newsletter highlighting our upcoming series releases and promotions!

Click on the Inside Romance link on the front page of **www.eHarlequin.com** or e-mail us at insideromance@harlequin.ca to sign up to receive your FREE newsletter today!

You can also subscribe by writing us at: HARLEQUIN BOOKS
Attention: Customer Service Department
P.O. Box 9057, Buffalo, NY 14269-9057

Please allow 4-6 weeks for delivery of the first issue by mail.

IRNBPA208

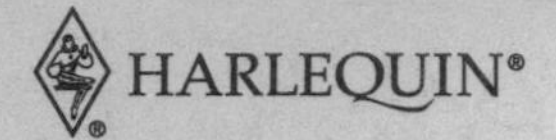

American★Romance®

COMING NEXT MONTH

#1245 ONCE A LAWMAN by Lisa Childs

Men Made in America

To protect and serve is the credo Chad Michalski has always lived by. But who's going to protect *him* from the vivacious blonde he just pulled over for speeding? Tessa Howard's recklessness has landed her in the Lakewood Citizens Police Academy, where the widowed cop can keep a close eye on her...and fight a losing battle against their growing attraction.

#1246 THE SECRET AGENT'S SURPRISES by Tina Leonard

The Morgan Men

Secret agent Pete Morgan has never considered himself a family man. Until he returns to Texas to collect his inheritance…and meets quadruplet babies in need of a home. To adopt the four tiny angels, Pete needs a wife. Prim, proper and wildly attractive Priscilla Perkins is the perfect candidate. Besides, it's just a temporary engagement. *Isn't it?*

#1247 ONCE UPON A VALENTINE'S by Holly Jacobs

American Dads

Single mom Carly Lewis thinks it's oh-so-ironic that she's organizing the local school's Valentine's Day dance! Cue the music *and* hunky Lieutenant Chuck Jefferson, the good-natured cop who wears his badge proudly on his chest and his heart on his sleeve. They've each been burned by love, so Cupid's working overtime this holiday to show these two how special they are together….

#1248 THE MAN SHE MARRIED by Ann DeFee

Maizie Walker is in a funk. After twenty years of marriage, all she wants is a little more attention from her husband, Clay. What's a girl to do? Make him jealous, of course! Maizie's convinced that flirting with another man will make Clay sit up and take notice. But when her plan backfires and Clay moves out, can Maizie ever get him back?

www.eHarlequin.com

HARCNMBPA0109